Death Broker

Ron Mueller

Death Broker

<u>Books and Stories by Ron Mueller</u>

<u>The Brian O'Neill Series</u>

Hawaiian Phoenix
Moon Curser
Death Broker

<u>The Taelo Series</u>

Taelo: The Early Years
Taelo: The Golden Feather
Taelo: Journey of Discovery
Taelo: Dangerous Passage
Taelo: Condor Clan Slingers
Taelo: Circumvention
Taelo: The Journey of Sages
Taelo: Collection

<u>A Taelo Story:</u>

White Swan and Quiet Pheasant
The Child's Name
Floating Cloud
Quiet Rabbit
Busy Bee
Little Otter & Talking Wren
Broken Spear
Burley Bear & Meadow Flower

<u>The Alex Evercrest Series:</u>

The River Front
The Girl on The Grill
Missing
Maggot
Racist
Votive Candles
Windy City
Country Road
Pool of Blood
Sins of the Daughter
Body Parts

<u>Other books by Ron Mueller</u>

The Door Series:
    The Door
    Delivery
    Journey Beyond
The Savitar Series:
    Journey's End
    Savitar
    Confluence
The Problem Solver Series
    Solutions
    Drug Lords
    Border Crosser
    Rhinos and Horns

<u>Single Science Fiction Books:</u>

Current Past and Future
The Event
The Door
Viajante 7

Imagination by Courtney Huynh and Chloe Parker

Ron Mueller

Death Broker
By: *Ron Mueller*

Around the World Publishing LLC
4914 Cooper Road Suite 144
Cincinnati, Ohio 45242-9998

This story is a work of fiction. Names, characters, places, and incidents either are products of the author's imagination or are used fictitiously. Any resemblance to actual events or locales or persons, living or dead, is entirely coincidental.

ISBN 13: 978-1-68223-984-1
ISBN 10: 1-68223-984-5

Distributed by Ingram
Brian O'Neill Model By: CURA photography @ShutterStock
Weapon by: DmyTo @ShutterStock
Tom Stone By: Pamela AU @ShutterStock
Cover Design by: Ron Mueller

Death Broker

Table of Content

Ron Mueller

Chapter 1: For the Love of …GUNS

In his youth Remi spent many hours with his father in his small gun shop. His father was in the gun repair business, and he also ran a gun shop that exclusively handled antique weapons. It was not a very lucrative business since the number of guns were few and the selling price very high. The occasional sale was always celebrated with a family outing or special dinner prepared by his mother. He loved the feeling that occasionally he got when he was allowed to handle these antique weapons. He had become quite talented at gun repair, the loading of shell and cleaning and polishing the various pistols and long guns.

That was all now a pleasant memory that always made him feel better.

He had recently become aware of someone checking on his business. One of his shop managers had described a young green-eyed man who had come in and asked him to show him some good pistols. He had shown him three different top end guns and had taken him to the one lane practice range behind the store to test the weapon. During their conversation, this person inquired about two other shops and their practices.

The shop manager said that the questions about the other shops were shops that were at the gun show, but he had not shared any information about them.

After that conversation, Remi decided to investigate who that person might be. He was not sure who this person was or why he might be interested, but he planned to make sure whoever he was he would pay a price if he screwed up the flow of money that was steadily going into his various bank accounts. He was not going to humor or coddle anyone investigating his doings.

He hired some mafia contacts to find out who was looking into what he was doing. He figured that they would have the means to discover who was mucking around his personal business. Once he knew who, he would confront them and see what was going on and take the action that was necessary. No matter what, he was not going to allow some individual to screw things up.

His biggest worry was the way he managed his gun sales business and whether some government entity was curious. He knew that he used every loophole and means to get around the gun laws. California had the toughest gun control laws. He had started his business expansion in California that had the toughest gun control laws. Though it had the toughest laws, it did not have the enforcement staff. They only managed to check about one percent of the larger gun shops and his gun stores most likely did not even make their radar screen.

His gun shops all operated on their own and the shop manager deposited his money into the bank at the end of each business day. He had purposely planned each gun shop to appear to be independent and separate.

He took his take in what he thought was a very sophisticated, open, semi-legal way. Each of his gun stores paid a consulting fee to a gun consulting organization that he had established. The gun shop business books were then managed in strict compliance with each state and US laws. The stores paid their taxes as required by law. Only he knew what happened to the consulting fee that was paid out.

He moved that fee through several US holding banks before sending it on to one of several offshore banks that ultimately handled and managed the money.

He had set up each of those banks with different unique identities. He had two US bank accounts on the west coast, two bank accounts on the east coast and two in the middle of the country. He figured that it would be impossible for anyone to figure out what banks and what accounts he had.

He adhered to a low-tech approach and did all his business transactions in person, via paper and in cash.

He utilized technology to make his life easier, but he kept most technology out of his business.

He had utilized his dark side connections to get six different passports and six corresponding driver licenses.

He smiled as he thought about the selection of the names of these six identities. He had used names that he had gotten off tomb stones in cemeteries in the city where each of the six US banks were located. Then he had his passport preparer make him a passport and driver's license using his picture but the names from the tombstone.

He then went to each bank and opened an account. Over the years, he came to enjoy the process of opening the next account. He had found out that he enjoyed the leisurely walk through the cemetery and the time he took to select the name from a tombstone. He always found seven names and then walked the route again before voting on which one he would select. He laughed as he thought about the fact that he had probably brought those people back from the dead to participate in a very different life than they might have had.

He stayed away from the large and sophisticated banks. All the US banks he chose were regional, local banks in smaller cities. He was interested in the banks only as a waystation for the cash flow that he generated so he maintained small accounts in each.

On a monthly basis he moved out five thousand dollars to the off shore banks that were managing his money. Each offshore bank had sophisticated investment management groups that then managed his wealth. He watched as year after year the money in these offshore accounts grew. It was a very satisfying and reassuring feeling.

The money he made once the money was offshore, he cycled back into the offshore account and never again paid taxes on it. This was one of the main reasons for having established them. His offshore accounts grew almost twenty-five percent each year.

So, his money was making even more money. He was acutely aware that it all started with selling guns.

Remi did not buy into the concept of the seller having any responsibility for how a weapon was used. He felt he was only responsible for the condition of the weapon at the point of sale. Most often he adhered to the local law but did not seek to follow it wholeheartedly. In fact, he supported several organizations that had either delayed the required background checks or had the background check law tied up in court to keep it from being enforced.

He additionally held gun shows and made a point of selling his guns as "antiques" to circumvent any required background checks. He figured if he were ever caught, he would apologize, pay a fine and move on.

He had spent much of his life fighting the bleeding hearts that thought that guns should be regulated and heavily taxed. His father had been a gunsmith who repaired guns and often resold the ones that were never picked up. He had listened as his father railed against the proposed restrictions on guns and had slowly taken the same position.

After graduating high school, he went to work in a small gun shop owned by a friend of his father. He was good at convincing prospective buyers to buy. When his boss decided to sell the gun shop, he was able to work out a deal to take over ownership incrementally by buying the owner out on a yearly basis. He modeled the purchase like people buy and pay for a car. This was what gave him a chance to get his foot in the door. He soon proudly put his name on the sign over the store's entrance.

He still had the ownership title to that first shop framed and hung up in his home.

Since the time of buying the first shop he had worked his way up the coast of California buying small gun shops. He then went on to cross the border into Oregon and then went on to Washington. It had taken him several years of steadily looking for the next gun shop.

He was not interested in large gun shops or franchised gun shops. He sought out the struggling mom and pop gun shops where he often found willing sellers.

He had each of his small shops operate independently. Unknown to those operating the gun shops they cooperated and supported each other because of the gun shows they participated in.

These were gun shows that he set up and ran near each shop on a rotating basis. He had a booth for each of his shops at each gun show. It made the gun show seem very large and diversified when in reality he owned every booth in the show. It did not matter to him when a potential buyer rejected a gun from one of the booths because they were not getting the discount they wanted and went to another. All the money ended up in his pocket.

All the people working at the booths worked for him and they all shared in a percentage of the final sales for that gun show. His stores were each run to maintain a profit and the gun shows generated a boost for the store hosting the one near their store. He and the managers of the stores thought of the shows as the icing on the cake.

The gun shows made a small fortune along the West Coast. It was a fortune that fueled his desire to make that fortune even larger.

He had then cast his eyes on the East Coast. He recalled the spring when he decided to follow the blooming of the flowering trees from Maine to Florida looking for and buying small gun shops. It had been an intense year but a very successful period. He followed the same slow and steady pattern of buying out small gun shops and getting each setup to be profitable. He made sure to keep the staff lean and the pay as low as he could possibly keep while maintaining a very low turnover.

He found that providing health care benefits was the key to keeping people working for him. He had each gun shop become a member of an Association Health Plan to make the insurance coverage available at a reasonable cost. His employees stayed because of this plan and the fact that he also added a profit-sharing plan to sweeten the pot.

He had reduced his staffing to the minimum and that staff worked hard but they were also rewarded well.

He had a soft spot for those that were at the bottom of the wealth ladder, but he had no qualms about making sure that he was at the very top of the wealth ladder. He had achieved being in the one percent and planned to stay there and continually move himself farther into that group.

He did a mental inventory of the homes and boats he now owned and decided that he had too many toys but in fact he enjoyed all his toys in slightly different ways.

He had a beachside home in San Diego that he considered his primary home since it was in the city where he had grown up. He had also purchased a sixty-foot sailing yacht that he had anchored at a dock at a top end marina.

He had a condominium in San Francisco on Knob Hill an area he and most other people considered the epitome of old-world elegance. He had a fifty-five-foot yacht not far away. He enjoyed walking the steep hills but often took a taxi back up to his condominium. He often walked to one of the many nearby great restaurants that graced that section of the city.

He had a home in Seatle that had a great view of Puget Sound and a fifty-five-foot yacht tied off on the pier that extended out from the edge of his property.

He had three beach side homes along the east coast from Maine to the southern end of Florida and either a power yacht or a sailing yacht that was associated with them.

And then there was his favorite location at the very southern point in Louisianna where he had a seventy-five-foot yacht on which he spent as much of his time as possible.

He had only one boat captain that traveled to the location where he planned to use one of his yachts. Each of his yachts had been purchased offshore and licensed offshore and he had not needed to pay any sales taxes. The cash he used to purchase the homes had all been transferred from his offshore accounts.

Once he owned the homes, he paid his property taxes with money held in his US banks. So, in essence, he straddled the tax laws as well as the gun laws. He still felt that, even with all these elaborate ways of avoiding taxes, he paid too much in taxes.

The next amazing money generating opportunity had occurred one day at a gun show where he met a person who wanted to sell him his collection of weapons. None of the weapons were registered and the owner needed the money to pay off some pending debts. He decided to buy the collection and offered just over twenty-five dollars per weapon.

It was then that he did some research and found out that there was close to four hundred million unregistered guns in the continental US. He began word-of-mouth advertising for those guns at each of his gun shows. He was amazed at how many weapons surfaced. He had to hurriedly set up a way to off load the weapons he purchased at a song.

He found a connection in Mexico and not long after his first truck full of weapons made its way across the border into Mexico. The next border he crossed was into Canada. He hit on a connection that provided a sea route to several countries. The rapid expansion of business had him buying guns from his various stores to fill the demand. He then smuggled them to the global hot spots. The money that he made from the transnational sales overshadowed the money from all his US gun shops combined.

He kept as low a profile as he could in this new market so that he would not get into conflict with the traditional gun runners.

During one transaction someone had given him the monicker "The Death Broker" and it had become the code name that he went by in all subsequent transactions. When someone wanted a supply of weapons, "The Death Broker" was often the one that fulfilled their request.

Those fulfillments each showed up as a huge inflow into his, gun runner, off shore bank account. This bank and the account was separate from all his other ones.

So, his worries about having someone investigate him were about them trying to find out how he had made his hidden fortune. He knew that most of his business growth money infractions were past the time where he could be charged with any laws that he might have broken but he didn't need anyone dragging his business out into the open and making his life difficult.

He had the connections, the money, the fire power, and the will to eliminate anyone that threatened what he had worked hard to establish. He intended to find out who was investigating him and once he knew the who and the why he would take the action necessary to protect what he thought of as his right and his to have.

There was no doubt in his mind that he would prevail.

Chapter 2: The Book Trail

It was a gorgeous morning on Maui. Annie was sitting in the shade of the pool side cabana looking out at the waters and working on her next painting. The girls were at school, Brian and Kekoa were working in the veranda searching for their next wayward billionaire. She had no clue how they would find such a person. She knew that so far Brian and Kekoa had made more money than she ever dreamt possible.

She had done exceedingly well as a painter and had made several million, but she knew that both Brian and Kekoa had more than one hundred million dollars each.

It was amazing to her that her millions had come from fifteen years of being a chained captive in the Pennsylvania forest and staying sane by focusing on painting, studying history and mathematics. Her abductor had wanted her devotion and love, so he gave her everything she asked for but her freedom.

She knew that her rescue by Alex and her recovery was nothing short of a miracle.

She had spent countless hours talking to her therapist, her parents and with Alex striving to get back into a world that had changed dramatically during the fifteen years she has been chained in the woods.

Alex was the person who had done the most to bring her back into the world. She had looked at all her paintings and had them put on the market for sale. She remembered fighting against doing that, but Alex had pointed out that she had two daughters to think about and to raise. That had made her think about the future. It turned out to be a good future.

Then to have found Brian and realize the first time that they had looked into each other's eyes that they were soul mates was a second miracle. His embrace of her, Linda and Laurie and his devotion to them from the very first time they met instantly bound their journey to each other.

Brian's story was very different. He had a sad start when he was young, and his mother died. Then Kaia and Koni had raised him as their own and he liked to say he had grown up in the gateway to heaven. What was amazing to her was that he had generated his fortune immediately the year after getting his law degree.

She thought of their experiences as the separate foundations that they each stood on, grew on and flourished. Their experiences were diametric opposites but somehow complementary.

Brian and Kekoa were joking back and forth about the fact that they were terrible hunters of wayward billionaires and that after more than six months they had not found the next one.

One morning during their target practice at the gun range Brian suggested they search the gun and weapons market for such a person.

Kekoa had replied that the gun market seemed to be a highly regulated market where it would be difficult to circumvent the law.

Brian agreed and said that such a market would be where someone who had figured out how to get around the law in some way would also most likely make a fortune. He suggested that they search for small independent stores since most of the large, syndicated shops or those in larger sporting goods stores would be owned by companies that would not be involved in circumventing the tax laws. They might use every tax loop hole, but they would focus on selling guns at the highest profit margin they could get gun enthusiasts to pay and they most likely would be successful.

Kekoa did a search for small gun shops in California. Once he had the list he decided to start in the southern part, hack into a shop's internet, and figure out the shop's computer connections. It did not take him very long and once he had made that connection, he figured out what bank the shop did business with.

Then he hacked into that bank's system and checked out the account for that gun shop. He then checked to see if the money in the shop's account was transferred to another bank. He was searching for where each shop's money went.

It was a tedious process that he had not been able to automate because of the high level of security most banks employed. He decided to just bear down and slug his way through it.

Brian suggested they select those gun shops that did business with smaller banks that might be less secure.

Kekoa was quite willing to narrow down the list of gun shops based on Brian's suggested criteria.

He did the analysis on about half a dozen gun shops and their banks. He shared the fact that the shops all seemed to have a clean relationship with the banks and vice versa.

He said that there was one shop that had a rather unusual consulting fee that was paid to an account in another US bank. He hacked into that bank and once he had that account, close examination showed that money being moved to yet another bank. He followed that money to yet another bank and then he found a connection to an offshore bank. The account at that bank showed the money being deposited on a monthly basis.

He let out a whoop and said that he had followed the consulting money trail from one small gun shop all the way to a bank in the Caymen Islands.

Annie heard the whoop and took the opportunity to say she was bringing out a pitcher of iced tea and that she had ordered a spaghetti Alfredo lunch with sides of asparagus and a small mixed salad. She suggested they gather at poolside, eat, and relax before the two of them once again immersed themselves in the hunt.

Brian gave a small laugh and thanked her for ordering lunch and bringing him and Kekoa back to reality. He jumped up and went to the edge of the pool, took off his shirt, made a shallow dive and took a couple of laps. He got out, dried off, put on his shirt, and sat down at the table. He felt rejuvenated.

During lunch Annie asked how the hunt was going.

Kekoa explained that he had traced money from one gun store all the way to an off shore account and added that now he would need to find another store where the money took the same route. He let out a groan and added that finding another would most likely be like looking for the next needle in a haystack and he was dreading it.

Annie asked if he could begin from the off shore bank and see if they had money coming into that account or another account from California and trace it back to some gun store or stores. She wondered if that might make things go faster.

Kekoa nodded and said that was a great idea and as soon as lunch was over, he would give that a try.

After lunch he was surprised at how many different sources of incoming money was coming from the same US bank and from that bank, he was able to locate the banks in California. He was then able to trace the money back to four additional gun shops. He was then able to verify that each of those stores was owned by the same individual.

He and Brian decided that they should try working backward from similar offshore accounts in the banks that their previously targeted billionaires had used in the Caribbean.

Kekoa agreed and said that he had experience with those offshore banks, and he would try the approach that Annie had suggested. That idea failed miserably; he got zero hits.

Brian suggested that they go to the first bank and see if there were other similar accounts that had monthly deposits coming in.

A few moments later Kekoa let out another whoop and said that he had found five more accounts with different customer names but similar cash flow profiles. He commented that only one led to a California gun shop, but the rest did lead to gun shops in Oregon and in Washington.

He then did a name search of the gun shops in those two states and found that they were all owned by the same individual. Kekoa said the issue seemed to be the fact that stores seemed to be owned by a different person when in fact it was most likely the same person using fake identifications.

Brian said that seemed to make sense. The person skimming money from these stores knew he intended to break the law and was trying to hide his identity by using different names.

Brian suggested they get a picture of the owner of the first store and then do some field work to see if the same person owned the other stores. He said that he would do the field work to see if the stores that they had so far identified were owned by the same person.

Kekoa made up the list of stores.

Brian said that he would plan a trip that covered all the potential stores and field verify the ownership. If one person owned all the stores, then they possibly had found their next target. However, Kekoa needed to tally up the amount of money that those stores had deposited to the banks in the Caribbean. He suggested that he also search for other banks that might have similar links to California, Oregon, and Washington State.

Because of the flight time to the mainland and the connection wait times for flights to Cincinnati where Annie and the girls had been living, Brian no longer used commercial flights. He called the private service that he had started using and arranged for his trip to San Diego.

He also rented a top end conversion van outfitted with twin sized bunk beds and a work desk that came with a driver that was offered by a small private rental company.

He figured that he would forgo staying at hotels so that he could travel as continuous a route as possible and not have to constantly be packing and unpacking a suitcase.

He felt the he needed to make the trip as fast as possible and get out of the field before anyone figured out what he was doing. He had the feeling that he had found the trail of his next wayward billionaire, and that this individual would be more of a challenge than the previous billionaires he and Kekoa had pursued.

He let Annie know that he planned to spend the next week or so going from the southern part of California to Seatle to verify the ownership of the stores that Kekoa had identified by using her suggested approach.

Annie, as always, gave him a hug and asked him to be cautious and that if this gun shop owner was a billionaire, he was most probably surrounded by gun toting people who might be very willing and maybe even eager to use their weapons to help him.

She added that he should make the trip as fast as possible, but he should get plenty of rest and eat well.

Brian agreed and said he would be very careful and try to keep his exposure to a minimum.

The next morning, once in the air, Brian decided to get some sleep so that he would be rested and ready to go when he got to San Diego.

The plane landed and taxied to a section of the airport used by private jets. The driver of the van met him there.

The driver, a dark haired, bearded individual with black eyes gave him the appearance of a bouncer versus a driver, introduced himself as Marvin Hester. He led the way to a large black van. He opened the side door and pointed to a cabinet in the back, a built-in twin sized bunk bed and a work desk behind the front seats that faced forwards.

He commented that when he was not driving, he would use the top bunk to get some sleep.

He suggested that Brian unpack his suitcase and set up his desk the way he might want it before they left the airport.

He then asked for the first address of where he was to go.

Brian took in the height of the van, the size, and the sparkling white interior. He noted that there was a fold down flap that would isolate the back of the van from the driver. When he asked about that, he was informed that this was to be used anytime when they were travelling at night and Brian wanted to use the desk area. There was even a space above the front area that served as additional storage space or an additional place for someone to sleep.

He got in and put his things away and put his brief case in the storage area above the desk. Then he gave Marvin the address of the gun shop located in the Pacific Beach area.

He got into the passenger front seat. He took note of a full-sized back seating area. Additionally, the front seat had a fold down work shelf. He also noted that there was a built-in cooler between him and the driver's seat that had cup holders on each side. He complemented Marvin on all the amenities built into the van.

Marvin said that it had cost him a small fortune but the trip they were on would take him out of the red. He added that he hoped to make the trip pleasant enough that Brian would be a happy return customer.

The drive to the first shop only took about forty-five minutes.

He asked Marvin to park on the side of the building in order to keep it out of sight. He got out and went into the back where he put on his Kevlar vest, put on his shoulder holster and a sports jacket. He then entered the gun shop and casually walked along a wall full of revolvers and then went over to the wall full of a variety of long guns. It was a small shop but definitely well stocked.

He approached the glass counter that featured some top end pistols and one AR-15. He spotted the type of gun that was in his shoulder holster. He decided to talk about it and two other models that were a few hundred dollars more expensive.

As he chatted with the person behind the counter, he learned that he was the only employee. The prices on the pistols were each written on a tag hanging from the trigger guard and Brian used the prices to discuss the values of the attributes of each pistol. During the discussion he extracted the name of the gun shop owner and the fact that the gun shop would host a gun show at the beginning of the following week. The clerk handed him a brochure that had the picture of the person sponsoring the gun show. It highlighted the fact that the show was a place to buy, sell or trade weapons.

The clerk suggested that if he were interested in buying one of the more expensive revolvers, they were looking at he should wait until the gun show because at the show he would be able to bargain for a reduced price.

Brian asked where the gun show would be held and learned that the large open field behind the shop would have a huge tent that would be put up as close to the shop as possible and parking would be on the other side. Brian thanked him and said that he planned to be at the show. He then walked out to the van and had Marvin leave by the exit that kept the van out of sight.

He asked Marvin to drive to the nearest restaurant. On the way there he sent the picture of the owner of the shop and the gun show schedule to Kekoa. He pointed out that it verified what Kekoa had found out and it linked that person to the offshore money accounts.

During the time he and Marvin were sitting and chatting over a cup of coffee, Kekoa texted back that there was no connection with the off shore accounts. He added that name came up at the small regional bank closest to the gun shop. He sent a picture of the person that he had found in a traffic ticket database. Brian returned to the van and got his computer down and turned it on. He took out his portable wireless travel printer and printed out the picture. He would have liked to have a color print, but he only had black and white, but he did have the color version on his computer and on his phone. The picture that Kekoa had sent and the one on the brochure the gun shop clerk had given him were the same.

He let Kekoa know that he had a match and that they should use the name that he had found at the bank.

He then asked Marvin to drive on to the second gun shop that was about seventy-five miles farther north. The stores that he was going to visit turned out to be roughly seventy-five to one hundred miles apart. They traveled north and Brian got into a rhythm of going into the gun shop talking to the shop owner and extracting all the information he could. He used the photo to verify that his "friend" really owned the gun shop.

Once he got to Seatle, he had Marvin turned around and head back to San Diego to attend the gun show.

He and Marvin were getting along well, and Brian liked the comfort of the large van. It indeed had save a lot of time and he was often in back either working or taking a nap

Once he was at the gun show he went in and realized that all the shops that he had visited were present. There were three booths more than the number of shops that he had visited. He focused on those three and got verification that they too had the same owner as the rest. He noted that the name changed for each state. So, he knew that the owner was trying to keep his profile low and separate.

The ability to have separate names and documents with those names meant that the person that Brian and Kekoa were following had the ability to generate multiple identities and had to have the necessary paperwork to support those identities. This was an individual that had his feet planted firmly on both sides of the line separating legal and illegal.

He sent the information to Kekoa and asked him to estimate the annual income for the number of gun shops that they had identified and to see if the names used in each state matched any accounts at the banks in the Caribbean.

Kekoa responded a few moments later and said that he estimated that it was close to fifty-five-million dollars a year. He added that the sites so far identified had on average been operating for ten years so they should have generated close to five hundred million.

He added that he had examined the off shore account and the bank that they had so far identified had close to that amount. He said that he bet they would find some additional offshore accounts, so he was bullish when he added that they had found their next billionaire.

Bryan agreed and said that he was on the way back to Maui.

He thanked Marvin for doing a great job and said that if there was another opportunity, he would have the return business he was seeking.

He got on the charter and slept for the entire flight back to Maui.

<u>Chapter 3: To the East</u>

After successfully setting up the series of gun shops up the West Coast, Remi felt flush about the cash flowing to his offshore accounts.

He had not expected to be doing so well.

He understood he was getting farther and farther into the illegal side of the gun trade. He was also confident that all the cash generated on that darker side was invisible to the US government and therefore he figured it was his to enjoy in any manner he saw fit and the likelihood of getting caught seemed very low.

He had recognized that more money could be made at each one of his gun shops by featuring the gear that gun owners would be attracted to. He had each shop feature unique gun accessories and go into the camping, clothes, shoes, and vests side of the business. The revenue from each of his gun shops ballooned.

His fortune was growing on all fronts, and he began thinking about how to expand his business.

He decided that he needed to see if he could establish gun shops along the East Coast in a similar fashion. Since it was spring, he decided to start his purchasing trek in Maine and work his way south along the Eastern seaboard.

His experience on the West Coast served him well. He knew the type of gun shops he was looking for and decided to go from small gun shop to small gun shop and test the desire for the owner to sell. He discovered that if the owner of the gun shop was older, that owner was more likely to be interested in selling.

Once he had a sales handshake, he gave that owner's name to the lawyer that he had hired in each state to handle the sales transaction.

He then moved on to identify the next gun shop. It took him more than a month to go from Maine to Florida. The trip generated fifteen East Coast gun stores and a potential income of about fifty million per year.

He was again doing better than expected and the cash flow streams were steady, and his accounts were all getting flush.

On the West Coast he had three separate personas that owned the businesses. He decided to only have three additional new ones to use as he went down the East Coast.

This made six different sets of passports and driver licenses he used in the US. He had two additional ones for the offshore banks he set up.

He laughed at the fact that the most difficult part of managing his gun shop empire was keeping track of who he was on any given day.

His birth name and identification was the one that was legally issued a US passport and the one he used in all his out of country travels. He used the other personalities with the banks and the individuals that he had hired to run each of the gun shops.

He traveled to Jamaica and Barbados to set up bank accounts to handle the money that he wanted to move offshore. Each of the banks offered a money management team to invest the money. He set them up and worked with them to have the accounts aggressively managed. He figured that he was already taking a much more personal risk and that being aggressive in how his money was invested did not bother him in the least.

He treated his Caribbean trips as vacations. He spent most of his time on the beach of the resort where he stayed, enjoyed taking a few dips and then sat and enjoyed drinks and watching the women in their skimpy beach wear as they strolled by.

The success of setting up another string of gun shops down the East Coast made him think about doing yet another expansion. A few months later he decided that he would make his last expansion by following the Mississippi river from its beginning to the Gulf.

Remi studied the map and decided to begin looking for small gun shops beginning at the Mississippi River head waters and then follow it down to New Orleans. He was surprised to find that the head waters was a point about one hundred miles slightly northwest of Duluth, Wisconsin. It was much farther north than he had expected.

The first gun shop he located was in the small town of Arago. It was a beautiful area with thick forests and hills that bracketed the small beginning of the Mississippi. The owner of the shop was ready to retire and pleased to have someone interested in purchasing the shop. Remi was able to get a good deal and connected the owner with the lawyer he had hired to handle the Wisconsin purchases.

He took the time to locate and hire lawyers in each of the states along the Mississippi River so he could get the purchases registered while he focused on finding the next shop to purchase.

As he traveled the twisting and turning of the small Mississippi, he was surprised at the large number of small gun shops that he found. Many of these gun shop owners were happy to share their books with him and then to sell the store to him. He found that many also volunteered to run the shops for him for at least three of four years. The made it much easier to keep the shops running and generating a good cash flow.

As he traveled south the number of gun shops thinned out and the owners seemed to get younger. He was sure that was his imagination, and he was acquiring more gun shops than he had planned. He, however, had the means to continue his purchasing as he traveled southward, and he did so.

He had traveled through fourteen states along the East Coast. There were five states on each side of the Mississippi. This gave him at least one gun shop in each of these ten states. In fact, he ended up with twenty-gun shops by the time he got to New Orleans. This was twice as many as he had planned but he looked at it as a way to generate twice as much money as he had originally planned.

He had purchased homes along the East and West Coasts but chose not to do so along the Mississippi. He figured six homes was more than he could handle or perhaps even use on any regular frequency. When he got to New Orleans, instead of a home, he bought the biggest of his seven sea going yachts. It was a seventy-five-foot-long yacht that featured a spacious front bedroom with a king-size bed and full bath. It had a full kitchen and two rear bedrooms. There was a front deck with an overhead canvass covering where he could sit and enjoy the breeze. It was a seventy-five-foot yacht that he fell in love with. He had the name "ESCAPE" painted across the back and on each side of the bow.

He then inquired as to the quickest way to get into the Gulf and leased a docking space in the southern part of Louisiana in a dock located on Grand Isle Beach.

He hired one captain that was willing to handle all his boats and travel as needed. The crew hands would always be hired locally. All he had to do was to designate which yacht he was going to use, and the captain would handle the rest.

He ended his middle of the country purchasing binge and went out into the Gulf to celebrate. He leaned back in his deck chair, looked out at the gentle waves, and enjoyed the breeze. He often wished that he had a significant other, but he seldom was lonely or really had any energy to change his situation.

He was a happy bachelor.

As the years progressed, his businesses all seemed to do well. There were periodic hiccups, but overall things went well.

Life was good.

Remi had enjoyed establishing his gun shop empire. It had now been in operation for almost five years, and it operated almost automatically.

He had established another business more by accident than plan. He had gotten into smuggling weapons from the US to areas that were eager to buy his unregistered weapons.

He had come upon this pool of weapons almost by accident at one of his gun shows. It was now making more money than all the rest of his businesses and it was all tax-free money.

Death Broker

He was known in that business as "The Death Broker." a
moniker that he felt mislabel who he was and he had at first been
offended, but it soon became evident that it gave him a
tremendous amount of influence. He then leveraged the aura that
it provided. He had no desire to seek more of that market than
came his way on request and the moniker seemed to help him
stay at a distance from other gun runners. He was content to be a
small fish in that dangerous pond.

He kept that part of his gun empire totally separated from the
others. The unbelievably large amount of money that flowed into
that one account significantly overshadowed his other accounts.
He purposely located that bank account in the far east.

The bank was in Bangkok. He was amazed at the cash flow
that almost immediately filled that account. He again set up a
financial team to invest the money and then stepped away. He
didn't need the money but loved keeping track of it.

He treated setting up the account as an opportunity to have a
vacation. While he was there, he took a multi-year lease out on a
condominium situated at the mouth of the Chao Phraya River
where it flowed into the very northern point of the Gulf of
Thailand. The condominium was on the top floor of the building
and had a large open veranda. The beach was just across the road
in front of the condominium.

He had the choice of going to the beach or swimming in the pool that was on the same level to the side of his condominium. He now had yet another unique view of the ocean and the pleasure of enjoying the sunset from his veranda.

He sat watching the sunset, sipping on a local white wine, and thought about his deceased parents. His father would have been amazed at the wealth he had accumulated, and his mother would not have believed it was possible that her lazy son would have done so well.

His stay in Bangkok was short and the long flight back to San Diego, though it was first class was excruciatingly long.

Over the years, he tried to spend some time in all the homes he owned. His San Diego home and his Gulf yacht was where he enjoyed spending most of the time. Once a year he took time to visit his Bahama and his Bangkok offshore banks to meet the financial management teams. He always took at least a full week's vacation while he was at each location. It was a comfortable way to run his business and rake in the cash.

Other than attending the gun shows that he sponsored most of the work to run the business was handled by his store managers, his accountants, lawyers, and his investment managers. He had arranged his life so that he was not tied up with the day to day but was still able to secure his future.

He had taken the time to go down the eastern seaboard attending the six gun shows that had been scheduled. He became troubled about the fact that one individual seemed to be asking questions about him and seemed to have figured out that he owned the shops under different names. He figured this person was going to cause him problems. He hired several detectives on the West Coast and several on the East Coast to find out this person's identity.

He also took the precaution of hiring two body guards. He then decided to get help from his contacts in several of the drug dealer gangs in case this mysterious individual were to stage an attack.

His other worry was that the attention was not coming from within the country but from some individual or organization that was involved in the black-market gun trade. Such scrutiny would mean that he might have stepped on someone's gun running toes. After some discussions with the ones, he had provided weapons, he concluded that was not the case.

He thought again about who might be interested. He figured the ATF would be interested if they suspected he was smuggling guns out of the country or being a gun runner supplying weapons to the world's numerous trouble spots. The other organization that might be interested would be the IRS if they suspected he was underpaying his taxes.

He came to the realization that he had no clue what he was facing and that the information he had hired others to find for him was excruciatingly slow to come in.

The decision of what to do was waiting on achieving some sort of sleuthing breakthrough. He was nervous but so far nothing bad had happened so there was nothing to react to.

Chapter 4: Expanded Search

Remi's unknown hunters were in plain sight. His guess about the IRS was close but even then, he was blind to the fact that he was looking at the people who were interested in him and they were slowly uncovering the extensive small gun shop empire he had built.

Brian and Kekoa were slowly slogging through trying to find which gun shops Remi had purchased. The learnings about the types of gun shops and banks that were used along the West Coast were helpful in getting them started in identifying the ones that had been organized along the East Coast. A significant difference was that they were looking in fourteen states along the East Coast versus only three states on the West Coast. This simple fact made the going slower.

Kekoa was able to identify three entities that were buying gun shops along the East Coast. This matched the number used on the west coast. He created a list of names and locations for Brian to check out.

Brian flew to Maine where he met Marvin who had driven his van there from the West Coast and had welcomed the repeat business. They traveled down the East Coast to verify that the three entities that Kekoa had identified were all Remi as he used three new identities as he purchased gun shops.

A new twist quickly surfaced for the search along the Eastern seaboard. The three new identities fell into place, the number of states increased from three to fourteen and the banks increased proportionally.

The identities were the easy part. Tracking the sales and finding out which lawyers were handling the sales was much more complicated.

Brian teased Kekoa when he listened to his complaint. He pointed out that he was sitting on a veranda on Maui most likely enjoying iced tea or lemonade while he was slogging his way down a series of small highways and out of the place small towns.

Brian visited the gun shops to verify Remi as the owner. He also visited the banks that Kekoa identified in each state. That meant visits to fourteen-gun shops, fourteen-banks and later some of the fourteen-gun shows that were part of the action. That put Brian on the road for almost three months.

Brian continued his use of the private charter. This gave him the fastest way to get from Maui to Maine and other East Coast sites. Even with the ability to fly comfortably, the trips took their toll. This was a period that he came to dread.

He arranged at least one week home between each of several trips that it took to cover the East Coast.

He first identified and visited each of the gun shops and at the same time visited the banks that they used. He covered one state at a time.

The gun shows based on their timing got added to gun shop and bank verifications. He made it a point of avoiding meeting face to face with Remi. Once he verified gun shop ownership, bank account linkage and the makeup of the gun shows he left the scene.

Marvin commented that the drive down the East Coast seemed to be more tedious than the drive up the West Coast. He commented that the roads they were driving down the east coast seemed more congested and had more cars on them than similar highways he had driven up the West Coast.

During his first gun shows Brian spent time getting the addresses of the gun booth presenters. These addresses accelerated Kekoa's search for gun shop ownership and banks being used and shortened his time in the field.

He was unlucky enough to have to do much of this during the winter weather but the fact that Marvin was doing the driving made a huge difference. He made sure that both he and Marvin took plenty of breaks as they made their way southward and into warmer weather.

Once Kekoa had the names and addresses of the gun shops he was able to identify the banks used and then he easily traced money transfers to two separate offshore banks. It took him considerable time to do all the hacking into the various bank systems, but his skill was up to it and he had been able to stream line some of the work. He commented that the case that they had chosen was the largest hacking case that he had experienced so far.

Kekoa noted that Remi had purchased three homes along both the East and West Coast. These six homes were all managed by separate property management companies. They were not rented out, but the management companies cleaned and maintained the homes. During the examination of the home information the ownership of three yachts along each Coast became apparent that these boats were managed by marinas near each of the homes. Kekoa commented at the wide extent of Remi's holdings and the amount of money that he must be making because he was also spending lavishly.

Kekoa visualized the information that had been gathered on a US map. So far, they had identified fourteen shops on the West Coast and fifteen on the East Coast.

Additionally, he had identified two offshore banks where Remi sent the money.

He commented that the gun sales must generate a significant profit margin.

It was during the visit to his last gun show that Brian was confronted by a person that he labeled as an enforcer. When asked for his identification, Brian gave his name as John Smith. He left that show knowing that Remi had gotten wind that he was being investigated. They had not been followed but he was sure that soon Remi would find out who was on his trail.

He informed Kekoa and asked if he could get into Remi's communication stream.

Kekoa said that he would get on it, but he needed to be in close proximity the first time to get linked with Remi's phone.

Annie noticed the effort Brian made to be present for all the family events. She knew that even with using the charter service, it added hours to his travels. She was glad that the cost of travel was not a factor. She thanked Brian for being so conscientious about being present at her art shows and at the various events Linda and Laurie were in. She loved his response that he scheduled his trips to the field around the family events. She knew the first time that she had looked into his eyes that he was the kind of person who thought and loved deeply. She was just as deeply in love with him and each of their interactions drove that feeling even deeper. She felt that life had finally rewarded her for her perseverance.

She did not enjoy cooking, so the family often ate the evening meal out at one of several of their favorite restaurants. They always did a family style of ordering and sharing. Kekoa was often at their dinners. These meals were centered around sharing each person's thoughts for the day. She made a point of getting everyone to speak about something they had done during the day. This became a part of every meal, and everyone came prepared to share.

Annie took note that Kekoa had started to bring dates to these dinners. It was clear to her that he was in search of a soul mate and that he was willing to entertain finding that person in any color and from any position in life. He always made a point of introducing the young lady and then during the individual sharing session he got that young lady to talk. Annie noted that what that young lady shared determined whether Kekoa brought her back to another dinner.

Then during one dinner, Kekoa introduced, Anela Kamaka, as a person he had known since his college days. She was from his hometown of Kalaoa on the big Island. He added that they had not known each other during their high school years but had dated briefly during their college years. She had recently been transferred to Maui by her company.

When it was her turn to share, she captivated the table as she told about the fun that she and Kekoa had in visiting all the historic sites on Maui and the great time they had when he tried to teach her how to sail board.

She laughed as she recounted feeling like she would easily accomplish doing it since she was a good surfer, but then she found out that it was different than the surfing at which she was good. She chatted smoothly with Linda and Laurie and seemed to fit in as part of the family.

She came to the dinners several times after that and not long after as they both sat next to each other holding hands Kekoa announced that he had proposed to Anela, and that she had accepted.

Anela proudly displayed a ring that she said was Kekoa's grandmother's engagement ring.

She let everyone know that they had agreed to wait a year and their wedding would be during the summer. It would be held on the Big Island in their hometown.

She made the point that everyone at the table was invited.

Brian suggested having an engagement announcement pool party and that he would spring for the event.

Kekoa agreed but said that he would like the party to be at his house but added that he welcomed Brian's offer to have it catered and setting up the entertainment.

Linda and Laurie asked if they could handle the catering and arranging the entertainment. They added that if they were allowed to invite underprivileged students, they could get extra credits that they needed to graduate.

Brian looked at Kekoa and asked what he thought of their offer.

Kekoa smiled and said that he was happy to have his younger sisters do such a nice thing. He was pleased to get a hug from both.

They immediately started to talk about which group they could get to play the music.

Two weeks later, Brian returned from his last trip along the East Coast so he could attend the pool party. He was somewhat exhausted and hoped to recover in the next two weeks.

The use of Marvin's services had saved Brian a significant amount of time, but it still took more than a month. He had split the month roughly into two, two-week periods and each time invited Marvin to return to Hawaii with him and spend a few days on the beach as a bonus for having now driven for two exhausting trips.

Marvin was ecstatic. The trip back to Hawaii, though on a private jet, still took almost ten hours but it did offer a level of comfort that could not be matched by a commercial flight. During those flights Marvin commented that he could grow to like traveling in such comfort and enjoy the good food and top service. He added that due to the good contract he had with Brian his rental service was enjoying a nice rise into the black. Currently his only concern was getting the van serviced.

Over the year, Marvin had virtually become another member of the family group. Anela introduced Marvin to one of her good friends from the big island. The two seemed to get along and sat for hours talking.

Annie smiled as she recognized the bloom of another romance.

On the conclusion of the East Coast verification, on the flight back to the island Brian thought about the pattern of a string of stores along each coast that had immerged. When he and Kekoa met the day after his return he suggested they check to see if there was a similar chain of gun shops down the center of the country.

It was no surprise to them to find gun shops that had been purchased in a similar fashion. This time Remi was alternating the ownership names between the identities he had used on East and West coast. It was clear the he was limiting the number of entities he wanted to use.

Brian said after a week off he would go from the northern most of the US gun shops in the middle and work his way south.

He got an enthusiastic agreement by Marvin to provide the driving service once again.

Marvin had a great interest in returning to Maui and said that he was researching the Hawaiian market for the type of service he wanted to provide on the islands.

Annie smiled and asked if there was more than business attracting him back to Maui.

Marvin smiled and replied that Hawaii had many attractions but the singular one that came to mind currently lived on the big Island. He planned to start his business there for that reason.

Annie nodded and said that would be a good place to start.

<u>Chapter 5: Amazement</u>

Annie let Brian know that Marvin had found love with Anela's friend Bailey.

Brian arranged with Marvin to be his driver along the Mississippi.

Marvin inquired whether there would be breaks every couple of weeks like the ones they had taken along the East Coast because he had great interested in returning to the islands during those breaks.

Brian chuckled and replied that yes indeed that would be how they would handle the trip. He asked if there was something in Hawaii that was of interest to him.

Marvin nodded and said that he saw his future as living on the big island and running a car rental service across all the islands. He added that he was sure he had found his soul mate and was going to do everything in his power to be near the person he had fallen in love with.

Brian smiled and said that was how he personally felt about living in Hawaii.

Marvin left Maui several days before Brian so he could drive his rental van to Minneapolis which seemed to be the closest airport to fly into.

Brian waited to hear from Marvin. A few days later Marvin let him know that he had arrived at Minneapolis and was ready for a drive down the Mississippi.

Brian left Maui and met him there.

He enjoyed the ride to the very beginning of the Mississippi head waters which was farther north than he had anticipated. The area was remote but very scenic and clearly a hunter's paradise. The large number of small gun shops did not come as a complete surprise. He did wonder if all of the shops made enough money to provide a good living for the owners.

He had perfected his approach to verifying Remi's name and identity. At the gun shows he was a friend of a friend of the owner and his interest was in one of the top-end weapons. He would chat about the guns and slide in questions about the owner. At the banks he identified himself as a DEA agent verifying the sale of the gun shop. The exchanges were always smooth and did not seem to cause any issues.

He soon realized that each of the ten states got an alternate of the six names that Remi used along the East and West Coast. It made sense to him that Remi had decided to limit the number of personalities he was going to utilize.

Brian figured between the six that Remi utilized for his US gun shops, two that he was using offshore and then the one that would be the official US passport. Remi had at least nine different personalities that he had to keep track of. Brian was sure that keeping track of where he was and who he was supposed to be was a challenge for Remi.

About half of the people managing the gun shops were the original older owners who were happy about selling their shop and then being able to continue operating it and earning a steady income. They were also happy that they were still banking with the same bank that they had always used and that their lives seemed to be more stable. The only thing that they said was that they no longer had any other employees that though it made easier on them, they had hated to let their employees go.

They commented that for them it was a perfect arrangement at a time in their lives when they were looking to slow down. They pointed out the they no longer handled the books, which made a great difference in how they managed the gun shop. Everything for them was easier.

Both Brian and Kekoa were impressed with Remi's knack of managing the shops in a manner that kept them in business, ensured satisfied employees and kept him out of the day to day running of the business. He had hired a single accountant to handle the books of all the stores and make the payments to the suppliers of guns and for any other services charged to the gun shops.

Kekoa was able to hack into the banks and get the information that linked each bank to one of the banks in the Caribbean. He commented that Remi had perfected his money laundering scheme and that the cash transfers were all below the level that would trigger an alarm as it was transferred. It was clear that Remi had set up his system so that each store had a steady stream of cash being transferred into the offshore banks.

All the transferred money that reached the off shore banks was on the accounting books as a fee to a consulting firm for the sales consulting service that was supplied. So even if someone were randomly inspecting the cash flow, it would not have raised a red flag.

Kekoa referred to Remi's method of skimming money to be sent to the Bahamas as a well-oiled machine or money going smoothly down a long water slide with the splash being the money accumulating at its end.

Brian then inquired about gun shows and learned the dates of the ones scheduled. He realized that Remi would have ten additional yearly gun shows down along the Mississippi River. This seemed to be equal to the ones along each coast. This meant that if Remi attended every show he would be almost continuously on the road.

Brian figured that Remi was probably very selective about which show he attended and let the other shows be handled by some managers he had hired to handle most of the gun shows. He most likely sat at home or one of his yachts to check in with the stores and the gun shows.

Midway on his trip he was lucky enough to hit one of Remi's gun shows that was being held in Missouri. He was able to visit all the gun shop booths of every store that Kekoa had identified. He discovered two shops that had not been on the list. He passed the information on to Kekoa who easily verified that they were indeed two that had been missed. Once he had the addresses, he was able to get all the details on the two and their linkage to a bank in the Bahamas.

Getting all the gun shop locations at that gun show allowed Brian to travel directly to New Orleans where the last gun shop had been purchased.

Marvin commented on their good luck and said it meant that they might get back to Maui earlier than they had planned.

Kekoa noted that Remi had purchased homes along both the East and West coast but had not done so in the middle of the country. He and Brian figured that Remi was partial to the ocean view and not so hot on the river view. They both agreed with Remi's preference.

In one of the home descriptions on the West Coast, highlighted the fact that a fifty-five-foot cruiser was included as part of the home sale. This caused Kekoa to see if there were other yachts purchased with the homes.

He was able to find two yachts on the West Coast and two on the East Coast. He figured that he might be missing a couple of yachts but figured that would come out when the IRS took the case and verified the details that he and Brian were gathering.

He decided to see if there were any yachts purchased in New Orleans. During his hack into the last bank that was located just outside of New Orleans, Kekoa spotted the sale of a very large and expensive yacht to one Remi Frensby.

He realized that Remi had not bought any homes, but he had bought a huge sea going yacht. It was the largest of the yachts that Kekoa had identified.

The information he was able to get on the yacht was more than impressive. It was absolutely the most beautiful boat that Kekoa had ever seen.

He then looked to see at which marina it was moored. The location was somewhat of a surprise to him because it was the southernmost point of Mississippi on the Gulf of Mexico. Kekoa thought about the location as one that was at the end of the world. He shared the find with Brian.

Kekoa put all the information that had been gathered on a US map. A total of forty-nine-gun shops, six homes and five yachts made an impressive display.

Brian commented that it had taken them more than a year of intense effort to generate the map of a gun shop empire that most likely generated one hundred fifty million dollars a year with much of that flowing into two offshore banks.

Kekoa commented that the offshore accounts seemed to indicate that money had been flowing in steadily for five to ten years and that Remi was indeed a wayward billionaire.

Brian declared that it was time to celebrate and figure out how to proceed to close in on Remi.

He then said that he wanted to get a look at the yacht that Remi had purchased. He and Kekoa agreed that he should visit the site where the boat was moored.

He asked Marvin to drive to the very southern tip of Mississippi.

Marvin drove to Grande Isle where the two checked into a beachside resort. They took a short walk along the beach and then they walked to where the yacht was anchored. Both were impressed with its size and sleek appearance. Brian commented that it would be great to go on board and get a first-hand look at the interior.

Kekoa surprised him and sent him a series of pictures that showed the interior of the yacht. They all agreed that it was a gorgeous yacht fit for a king.

After enjoying the beach for another day, they returned to New Orleans and Brian took the charter flight back to Maui.

Marvin stayed behind to drive his van to San Diego. He left with a smile on his face when Brian gave him the date that the private jet would return to San Diego and fly him to Maui.

Brian figured that he and Kekoa had enough information and evidence that would ensure that the IRS had sufficient facts and detail with which to build a fool proof case. Brian's time in the field had been extensive and he was ready for a break.

He now looked forward to a wrap up of the information and then the arrest of Remi for money laundering and tax evasion. Neither a tax evasion nor a money laundering case was glamourous. Neither would draw any national news, but they were very airtight cases that the IRS loved, and they were cases that kept he and Kekoa invisible and on the sidelines. This was exactly where he wanted them to be.

He and Kekoa had discussed how to turn over the case to the IRS contacts that would handle the cases. The decision by the IRS was that they planned to make the charges in Cincinnati since that would be central to all the various gun shops and any witnesses that would be called.

Brian and Annie liked the idea of the case being judged in Cincinnati since it would give them the excuse to visit their friends there.

It took both he and Kekoa two more months to organize all the information that they had accumulated. Kekoa commented that it was a bigger outrigger than he had anticipated paddling.

Brian laughed and added that it was a "humdinger o ka hihia," and it certainly did not fit into any outrigger that he had seen on the island.

Neither of them had any idea of that their wrap-up effort would discover an astounding piece of information that would make the case even bigger than what they had already embraced. It would totally change the nature of how they saw and thought about Remi.

56

Chapter 6: Realization

Remi was sitting comfortably under the canopy on his largest yacht that he had named "Escape." The name signified that it provided him an escape from his everyday tensions generated from the business he was in. The Gulf waves were gently hitting the bow giving the yacht a gentle rocking motion. The fishing was good, in fact it was better than usual. He was sitting and slowly reeling in his line waiting for the next hit. The light blue morning sky was speckled with scattered cumulous clouds that reminded him of the childhood game he used to play identifying various animals or other shapes that he would identify. He had not thought about his childhood for quite some time. It had been a somewhat mixed experience. He had been very close to his father and somewhat removed from his mother, but both had been good parents. He had only good memories about the two of them.

His mind was less focused on fishing and more on the fact that some unknown individual was investigating him and his business. He thought of it as being stalked. He was frustrated by the lack of progress that his private investigators had made in finding out who this person was. He had hired three investigators but so far, they had produced nothing. He was about to give up on them.

He had taken the precaution of hiring two personal bodyguards to make sure that he had the protection he might need. He was an expert marksman, but he figured that having the extra protection was worth it. The bodyguards had been recommended by one of his underworld contacts as two persons that were deadly and who were willing to engage in a gunfight if necessary. He had been surprised when he met Ray and Jerry. They looked almost like brothers. To him they seemed rather young, both had blue eyes and were blond. They did not fit the caricature that Remi had projected of a bodyguard. They looked more like two college sports jocks that were enjoying the life they lived.

He was sitting a few feet from Ray and Jerry as they seemed to be enjoying the fishing more than he was.

A few moments later, he was in the middle of reeling in another fish when his phone rang. He was going to ignore it, but the ring let him know that it was from his underworld contact. He handed his pole to Ray and took the call.

The call made his day. He learned that the person that he was interested in was a young lawyer named Brian O'Neill who resided on Maui. The contact said that as far as he could tell this person was in private practice, but he did not have an office on Maui. The contact went on to explain that he had not found out who the lawyer's clients might be. He pointed out that this O'Neill, though young seemed to be doing quite well.

Remi figured that someone must have hired this O'Neill for some purpose. He could not figure out who might have that much interest. He wondered what this O'Neill had found out about his business and what he had passed on to the person that had hired him.

He called up his two investigators and instructed them to find out what O'Neill had found out about his business. Not long after he got calls from them and let him know that several of the gun shop managers had talked to an individual that seemed interested in who owned the gun shop, but they did not have a name nor any specifics.

He had no idea how much this O'Neill might know or what anything that he had seen or learned would mean to those who had hired him. His inquiries into what O'Neill had asked about or had been interested in did not surface any additional useful information.

He went down the list of the various people he knew or was aware of, trying to figure out who might be interested in his gun business. The bulk of the gun business was controlled by large outdoor camping sports shops that would not care about the small gun shops.

There were only a few individuals in the gun selling business that were competitors so he decided to see which ones might be trying to figure out how he ran his business.

He decided to redirect his investigators to check out the half dozen people that might be interested.

Remi shook his head as he thought about the situation. It just did not make sense. This was a situation that he had never anticipated or envisioned. It left him feeling somewhat inadequate and mystified.

He called it a day and had the boat return to the dock. He figured that a good workout would help his thinking. During his workout on the treadmill and some light weightlifting he decided that he would go to Maui and check out this O'Neill himself. He wondered if he should just confront him and ask what his client's interest in him might be.

He did a quick online search on Ryan O'Neill and where his home on Maui was located. He was surprised to find that it was located overlooking a golf course fairway and that the hotel where he had made his reservations was directly on the beach below O'Neill's home.

He marveled at how easy the search had been. He ran his name through a similar search and was dismayed to find that if he put in the location to search for his name the system would find his home or at least the homes of anyone with a similar last name. He then wondered who had spent the countless hours it had taken to put that information online.

A few hours after he made his reservations at the hotel in Maui, he arranged for a private flight there. The hotel was on the beach, and he had made sure that the suite he had reserved had three bedrooms.

He informed Ray and Jerry, who were very enthusiastic about the trip and wondered how long they would stay and if they were going to go to the beach while they were there. They both commented that neither of them had ever been to Hawaii.

Those questions caused Remi to adjust his packing to include his swimsuit and his snorkeling equipment. He had once tried scuba diving but was too phobic about being under so much water. He asked Ray and Jerry whether they had snorkeling equipment. Neither did so he sent him out to buy some.

He then decided to also take his golf clubs. The trip was taking on a slightly different character than his initial intention. He had no problem having a good time even if his intention were to do some serious investigation.

He scheduled the flight to leave in the very early hours of the morning so that the arrival time had them landing close to the lunch hour. He checked out the hotel's lunch menu and decided that the hotel's restaurant would do. He figured he would later look for additional restaurants that might be of interest.

He had been asked what size and model of private jet he desired. After looking through the six planes that the service offered, he selected one of the smaller planes. He thought the plane he had selected had a mask like one of the comic book superheroes. The front half of the plane was white on the top half and black on the bottom. Its superhero mask was a dark blue one that went around the front cockpit windows.

He marveled at the plane's interior. The carpet was a dark blue and all the seats were white leather. There was one serving table with two chairs facing forward and the other two facing the back. There were also separate seats that were able to open to a flat position.

Ray had been able to drive up to the plane and the two pilots and the attendant loaded all the luggage.

He and Jerry went on board where they were asked about their meal and drink preferences.

He took the back seat of the four that faced forward. The attendant immediately offered him the selection of drinks, snacks, and meals that were available. The menu featured a nice variety of choices.

He had been surprised at what he thought was a reasonable price for securing the services of a private jet and continued to be surprised at such good service and such luxury.

Once Ray returned after parking the van, the pilot came back and shared the flight plan and the time it would take for the flight. He suggested that they enjoy the great service and the choice of meals. He added that it had been a slow month and the crew serving them was rested and they were the best.

It was a smooth take off. He was asked what music he desired to listen to. He let Ray and Jerry choose the music.

He sat enjoying some hot mocha and nibbling on an ultra-buttery scone with a hint of sweet strawberry tanginess.

He watched as Ray and Jerry gobbled down several scones, ate two eggs and had two pancakes. They were joking and laughing about how great their job was.

It was clear to him that both would need to do lots of walking, swimming and more to get rid of all the calories that they would most likely consume on the trip.

He thought about the fact that his young bodyguards had chosen a line of work that would likely place them on the outside of most long-term, family-oriented relationships. It might also include a short life.

He decided to take a nap and adjusted his chair to a flat position that kept his head slightly up. He came awake hours later as the plane made a slight bump on landing.

This he thought was how travel should be managed.

The car and driver that he had hired came out to the plane and once all the luggage was loaded, they drove across the Island to the Wailea, Makena area where the hotel was located. The hotel was one of the top luxury hotels on the island and featured a wide variety of amenities. The excellent check-in service matched the price that he was paying for the three-bedroom suite.

They were escorted to the suite and given a tour of all the unique features. He was pleased that his bedroom and the common living room area had great views of the ocean. The two additional bedrooms had a view of the pool area and the more distant mountain ridge where a number of wind turbines ran up its ridge. He figured that the view made the room one where he could relax during the early evening.

After settling in, he went down to the restaurant that featured a Hawaiian based menu. Once again, the service was top end, and the menu selection was extensive. He had to ask about various Hawaiian dishes and finally selected a ribeye prepared in a Hawaiian style. He continued his exploratory lunch by ordering Hawaiian Coleslaw, purple sweet potatoes, and pineapple fried rice.

He selected a sparkling pineapple wine which did not meet his red wine with red meat practice, but he figured he would go with it anyway. He was not disappointed by its slightly sweet hint of pineapple flavor.

He noted that Ray went for the Hawaiian pork, baked beans and a potato mac salad. Jerry went for a rack of lamb, a side salad, and asparagus spears. He was pleased to note that both ordered an iced tea for their drinks.

He made a point of eating slowly and enjoying the unique flavors of the meal.

He asked Ray and Jerry what they thought of the hotel and the food.

Both commented that they felt like kings and that the food was great.

After lunch he took a walk on the wide walkway in front of hotel. It seemed to run the length of the beach.

When he returned, he arranged to go for a drive. He wanted to drive by Brian O'Neill's home.

It turned out the home was just on the other side of a golf course from the hotel in which he was staying. He commented that this Brian O'Neill lived in a very upscale neighborhood. He wondered what a thirty-something-year-old lawyer did that earned him the kind of money that it would take to live in a Maui gated home that overlooked a golf course. There was a six-foot stone wall with an entrance gate on the street side of the home. As they drove very slowly by the driveway gate, he was able to see the rose lined drive leading to a four-car garage area. He decided to go back to the hotel room and google out the home and get both an inside as well as an arial outside view.

He arranged with the driver to have him return to O'Neill's house and sit on the street. He instructed him to follow any male that exited the home but only to note any other people coming or going.

He went up to his suite and got online to scope out the home. He was surprised to find that he could not get an indoor view of the home. This made him even more curious about O'Neill. He was a person with enough influence to get the indoor view of his home blocked. That indicated that he had some sort of significantly influential connections. This made Remi's concern go up another notch.

The overhead satellite view clearly showed a full-size pool area with a wide veranda that went halfway around the home. The house was at the edge of the number nine fairway. It clearly was the home of a successful person. Remi knew that it was more than most thirty something lawyers would normally be able to afford. The more he learned the more worried he was becoming.

In the late afternoon, he got a call that a red sports car that had four people in it was leaving the house, and that his driver was going to follow to see where it would go. Fifteen minutes later the driver called and said that the car had gone to a nearby restaurant where he had watched four people exit the car and go up the stairs to the restaurant.

Remi got the name of the restaurant and made a reservation. He had the driver return to pick the three of them up.

As he walked into the restaurant, he looked around the tables to see if he could figure out which group might be the O'Neill group. He was led to an outdoor table where he found himself facing one family group that was at the corner of the restaurant veranda area. He watched as a very tough looking individual wearing a shirt that had the words Big Island across a picture of that island on his back enter and sit down with them. It was clear that this person was friends with everyone at the table.

He noted which waiter was serving the table. He decided to see if he could learn the family's name.

Brian recognized Remi as he was led to the table. This put him at full attention. When Kekoa arrived, he let him know and asked him to sit at the end of the table so he could also keep an eye on Remi and the two younger men. One had his back to their table and the other was sitting next to Remi periodically looking their way. He commented that the two younger men were most likely bodyguards and armed.

He let Kekoa know that he was armed.

Kekoa commented that he had his weapon in the pouch he was carrying.

Annie caught the gist of what was happening and asked if she and the girls should leave.

Brian thought for a minute, shook his head, and said that they were being observed but he was not sure that Remi knew what he or Kekoa looked like.

He watched as Remi went to the back corner of the veranda where the waiters were gathered and had a conversation with the waiter serving their table. The waiter turned to look at their table and said something to Remi. He watched Remi press a bill into the waiter's hand and then return to his table. He figured that Remi now knew who he was looking at.

Brian and the family were regulars, and he knew the waiter by name and even knew that he had two daughters about the same age as Linda and Laurie. When the waiter returned, he quietly asked him what size tip he had been given by the gentleman who had tipped him for getting his name. He was not surprised to learn that it was a hundred-dollar tip.

He smiled and asked the waiter what drink the gentleman had ordered. He then asked the waiter to serve that person another and let him know that Brian was aware of who was watching him. He then pulled out two one-hundred-dollar bills and put them in the waiter's hand. He smiled and added that it might help ends meet.

The waiter thanked him and said that he hoped that he had not caused his best customer any problems.

Brian smiled and replied, "a'ole maika'i loa,"

Luarie smiled and said that she understood it to mean that all was well.

Kekoa congratulated her on learning Hawaiian.

Everyone at the table was now aware that they were being watched. Linda commented that it was exciting. Laurie agreed and said that she was going to go to the bathroom so she could get a good look at who was watching them. Linda said that she was going to go too. The two stood up and turned to go to the restroom that was inside near the other end of the veranda. They were joking and laughing as they walked slowly back and past the table where Remi was sitting.

Annie quietly commented that Brian was a bad influence on the girls. They were becoming adventuresome exactly like him.

Brian smiled and replied that it all came with the package that she had embraced.

Linda and Laurie returned and commented that the bodyguards were quite handsome.

Brian smiled and said that he didn't doubt it and he didn't doubt they were as deadly as they were handsome.

Laurie nodded and said that she bet she could take either of them out with the skills she had so far achieved in her martial arts class.

Kekoa chuckled and said that though he was sure that was true any interactions with the bodyguards would most likely involve bullets from their guns and not a karate move.

The waiter raised his tray to let Brian see that he was delivering the drink. He then set the drink down in front of Remi and pointed to Brian.

Brian raised his glass and watched Remi raise his in return.

The connection between them had officially been made.

Chapter 7: Discovery

Remi smiled, he realized that the person he had been trying to identify was informed, intelligent and well versed. He also seemed to be very confident as indicated by him having bought him a drink. He decided that he would enjoy his meal and just observe the people around O'Brian. He realized that the young man enjoyed a close family relationship and the person that he thought of as a bouncer was a close friend. He smiled when he thought about the two young ladies with their backs to him and the fact that they had most likely walked past his table to get a better look at him, Ray, and Jerry. He also realized that O'Brian had done his homework and knew him by sight. Though he was impressed he was now even more worried. His adversary did his homework and had obviously done the field work. He wondered how many of his stores and gun shows he had visited. He wondered about the role of the person at the end of the table. He was certainly a tough-looking individual that seemed to be a close friend.

The only other thing that struct him was that the woman with long blond hair at the table was beautiful. Her smile had a contagious effect. It was clear that she was guiding the discussion at the table and seemed as confident as Obrien. He concluded that he was looking at a very close family.

The two young girls had caught the eye of his two young bodyguards who had commented that they were quite beautiful but too young.

Brian looked at Kekoa and said they had a lot of homework to do and that it was time to close the case.

Kekoa nodded but did not say anything. He was instead focused on getting his computer out and turned on. He put it on a small table at the side of the main table. He activated his phone number capture routine so if Remi activated his phone, he would be able to capture his phone number and the number that Remi was calling. This was the reason he had been late. He had stayed behind because he was in the middle of finishing the program when everyone went off to the restaurant.

Remi made the mistake that Kekoa had hoped for. He had decided to call it an evening and called the driver to bring the car around.

Kekoa smiled as he saw his hacking routine capture the numbers. He looked to Brian and said that they had connection to Remi, raised his glass and made a toast of success, closed his computer, and put it in his bag.

Brian congratulated him, smiled, and said that he had earned an extra strip of bacon with the breakfast of his choice.

Laurie laughed and said that when she went to work, she hoped to get a better thank you bonus than an extra strip of bacon.

Kekoa shook his head and said that it was not about money but about having a superb breakfast cooked by the best partner one could work with.

Annie nodded and agreed that the two of them had so much money that she wondered why they were still working.

Laurie exclaimed, "Mom you have made millions with your paintings why do you still paint?"

Annie nodded, smiled, and said, "because painting is in my blood, and I love to do it." She then added, "My daughters are getting too smart."

Linda shook her head and said that her younger sister was not getting too smart but was just being a smart aleck.

Brian was only half listening as he watched Remi stand up, raise his glass, then leave by the door behind him instead of walking by the table where they were sitting.

He looked at Kekoa and asked whether he could now keep track of Remi.

Kekoa nodded and said that as soon as they got back to the house, he would check on his location. Then the two of them needed to decide how to handle the situation. He commented that they did not want a repeat of the assassination attempt that Maite had set up on their last case.

Annie nodded and said that Kekoa had hit the nail on its head, but they should finish their dinner and then enjoy desert.

Before leaving the restaurant, Kekoa activated the phone location program and checked Remi's location. Once he had that information, he said they should still be cautious when they left the restaurant.

He said that he had driven the black van, and he would get it and bring it to the exit. Then Annie and the girls should come out. He added that Brian should be the last to come out. He said that they should leave the red sports car and retrieve it later.

Kekoa did not wait for agreement but went out to get the van. He was cautious and ready in case he had misjudged the situation. He got to the parked van and drove it to the restaurant's exit. Everyone made their exit. He drove slowly to the house. He drove the van into the garage and closed the door. Everyone got out and thanked him for being the driver and getting them home safely. His fourteen-year-old car was sitting in the fourth garage stall where it normally was parked next to Brian's even older car in the third stall.

The sparkling red convertible that Brian used for family drives was normally parked in the second stall which at the moment was empty since it was back at the restaurant.

They all went in. He and Brian went up to their second-floor office and spent a few moments organizing what they should do in the next couple of days. They concluded that they should close the case and turn it over to the IRS. They also realized that because of the locations of all the gun shops, the US banks, and the offshore banks the case sprawled across the country and most likely multiple IRS regional districts.

They decided that they would keep a close eye on what Remi was doing and work to organize the information they had so it could be easily turned over.

After Kekoa left to go home, Brian went down to the family room. The girls were sitting at their study desks doing homework and Annie was working on one of her paintings. He figured he would do some reading. He asked if anyone wanted any refreshments. He got a response from them that they were OK. He then sat down with his cup of green tea and opened the book that he was halfway through reading. But reading did not seem to take, instead he was thinking through what he and Kekoa needed to do to turn over the case to the IRS.

Just across the golf fairways, Remi was doing a fast-paced walk on the treadmill in his suite and thinking through what he should do. He decided that he would spend a couple more days seeing if he could get more information about O'Neill and his family. The girls looked about the age that put them in junior high school. Perhaps he could find out where they went to school and learn more about the person that he considered an adversary.

The next day he visited both junior high and high schools, but he did not find any O'Neill children. At the end of the day, he was frustrated and ready to throw in the towel at trying to be an investigator. He had no clue what to do next. He thought about confronting O'Neill but was not sure that would do any good. He figured the only thing he would do was to find out if this person were as formidable as he seemed.

He decided to spend one day just being a tourist. He called around and found a yacht that he could hire to go out fishing and to catch the sunrise and the sunset on the following day. After spending the day out fishing, he planned to have dinner in the evening. Then on the next morning he would play a round of golf and in the late afternoon he would take his charter and return to Louisianna and go and enjoy a few days out on the Gulf on his yacht.

The morning after the dinner where Remi had shown up at the restaurant, Brian and Kekoa discussed the best way to close the tax evasion case against him. Kekoa suggested they develop a clear, visual depiction of how the money from each of the small gun shops was handled. He said that each of the gun shops sent thirty percent for services rendered to an intermediate US bank that then sent it to an offshore bank. He made the point that the only services rendered by this straw company, which was owned by another fake company, registered to Remi, was a monthly letter that highlighted gun articles being published by various gun magazines. There was nothing that could be used by the gun shops to improve their business. It was simply a way to skim thirty percent off the profits from each small gun shop. That thirty percent when taken from more than forty-five-gun shops amounted to a significant amount.

Brian suggested they quantify the small cash flow streams that each gun shop represented and create a diagram that they could present to the IRS. He added that the way they had turned over their material in the past had aided the IRS to greatly accelerate the prosecution of those cases.

They spent the rest of the day creating a detailed map of the location of each gun shop. it's average monthly gun sales, the profit from the sales and how the cash was then flowed on its way to the Bahamas.

The information surprised them as they realized that their thirty percent skim estimate had to be significantly low. It turned out that after their payment for the services to the offshore company, each shop was only making a seven percent margin on their gun sales. This meant that ninety-three percent of the profit was going directly to the three offshore banks. Those three banks in turn sent ninety percent of the money to a fourth offshore account where it was managed by an investment group.

The next surprise was the amount of money that made that trip. It was more than just gun sales would support. On closer examination, Kekoa noticed that after Remi purchased a gun shop, it began to heavily advertise specialty gun equipment, sporting clothes, and camping gear as well as specialty and antique weapons. These items had a higher profit margin than general gun sales and it was clear that the advertisements had an almost immediate positive impact on the sales of each of the shops.

He highlighted this and commented that Remi should have stuck to the honest handling of his money and just paid the taxes because he would have been making a ton of money because of his astute handling of the gun shops. He had tripled the sales and profit margin of each of his shops! He could have accumulated much of his wealth in an honest fashion.

Brian shook his head and said that the amount of money in all the banks and the money in the final account still did not make sense because there was still more money in that final account than the various gun shops would have generated.

He commented that they had missed something and that there was money in that final account that did not come from the gun shops.

Kekoa looked at the numbers and said that he needed to do a detailed look at each of the banks to see where he had missed additional money showing up.

The cash flow from each of the banks in the US was easy to examine and confirm. He found that there was nothing that needed changing.

Kekoa said that the money flowing from the gun shops to the offshore account balanced out to the amount that was found offshore but the money for the purchases of the homes and the boats did not show up anywhere. There had to be another source of money that they had missed.

Brian asked how much of a gap there seemed to be and when Kekoa finally answered they both let out a groan.

Kekoa frowned and then said that there seemed to be a two hundred-million-dollar gap. He said that he would need to trace the money used to pay for the homes and the boats. The cash flow for these purchases did not come from the cash flow from the various gun shops.

It took him several days of hacking to trace each of the home purchases. He focused on the purchase of the first home and boat and worked for several days to get into the bank's account to learn from where the money to pay for the house had originated.

When he more closely examined the offshore banks, he immediately identified that there were additional deposits that came from various other banks from a variety of countries. He groaned and said that their large case had just taken on a much larger scope.

He commented that Remi might be a global gun runner and distributor.

He highlighted that money that had originally come in from Mexico and Venezuela had stopped after a few years. He then went into both the Mexican and Venezuelan banks and discovered that they were now sending the money to a bank in Bangkok, Thailand.

When he tried hacking into the bank there, he ran into a much more sophisticated fire wall. He called his mentor back in Cincinnati, Johnnie, for help.

When Johnnie followed the Kekoa's hack. He chuckled and commented that the bank in Bangkok had one of the most sophisticated firewalls he had seen to date, but he figured that they could fool it by imitating a bank that was transferring money in. They needed to use a US bank to transfer in a sum of money. He asked if Kekoa had a hundred thousand dollars that he could lose to get into the bank in Bangkok.

Kekoa asked Brian whether he was willing to burn a hundred grand to get to Remi's Bangkok bank account.

Brian shook his head in the affirmative and chuckled and said that his partner was a very heavy gambler.

Kekoa let Johnnie know that it was a go.

Johnnie guided Kekoa in setting up the opening hack and then instructed him on how to keep the door open long enough to find Remi's account and the amount of money in that account. He had to put a shoe in the hack-door to keep it from totally closing by dribbling in the hundred thousand dollars, one penny, one day at a time.

The more than twenty billion dollars they found in the account made all the work that they had done so far seem insignificant. The two hundred million that they had thought was such a large amount of missing money was suddenly insignificant.

Brian laughed and added that it was a "humdinger o ka hihia" of a discovery and overshadowed all their hard work up to this point.

They agreed that they needed to track down the source of the money that had periodically been sent to the Bangkok account. So much money meant that Remi associated with some of the top suppliers of weapons to the various world trouble spots.

It was a side of the business that neither Kekoa nor Brian had envisioned.

Kekoa commented that Remi might be as big a gun runner as Whitey Bulger or Victor Bout two of the more prolific gun runners in US history.

Brian said that it surprised the Bejesus out of him.

Kekoa smiled and asked him if he had picked up that saying when he had been in Ireland going to school.

He examined the money being transferred in from the Mexican bank and concluded that Remi was doing a very significant business in smuggling guns into Mexico. Whoever was buying them there was most likely some of his biggest customers.

He verified that Remi did not have a license to ship or sell weapons into Mexico or any other country.

He pointed out that the sources of money entering the Bangkok account meant that Remi was a transnational seller of weapons to a variety of countries as well. Those countries, all around the world, were in daily news reports highlighting the fighting that was happening.

Brian said that their case was now more than just a failure to pay taxes that involved the IRS but also one that involved the ATF and potentially the FBI. He added that this was a case the two of them would want to stay as close to the outer edge of as possible because a deep involvement might take up years of their lives.

Kekoa agreed and said that he would focus on getting the information as clear as possible so they could present a clear investigation path for all US agencies that might end up having some sort of involvement.

He commented that he wanted his life to be spent with his soul mate and enjoy living in the Hawaiian paradise.

<u>Chapter 8: Misfire</u>

The sun had not yet come up over the horizon as Remy sat on his yacht taking the first bite of his butter and syrup covered pancake with a poached egg on top. He planned to do a little fishing and then enjoy sitting in the sun to improve his suntan. He found that his time out on the yacht was what he enjoyed the most. He had come to the realization that he no longer enjoyed going to gun shows where it seemed he ended up talking with one dimensional men who had a macho attitude and acted as if they had a right to be rude and obnoxious.

Remy felt bad about his decision to eliminate this O'Neill lawyer, but he knew he would feel worse if he did not act. O'Neill seemed to have a great-looking family life, but he had made a very bad decision when he chose to muck around in his gun business. He was sure that whoever had hired him was not paying him enough and now he had decided that his remedy was to make him pay the ultimate price. He smiled as he thought about the fact that he had the money, and he would do what needed doing because he was worth doing it for.

He contacted his mafia connection to get the name of a top assassin he should hire. He insisted he wanted the best and someone that delivered results as promised.

He contacted the suggested person though he did not get to talk to him but exchanged a series of messages. He was surprised to find that it would only cost him two hundred thousand dollars. He had expected it to be closer to ten times that amount, and he would most likely have paid it.

He liked the payment arrangement since it would be an all-cash transaction. The payment was to be paid in cash that was to be mailed to a post office box address in a series of small amounts. Two thirds of the cash had to be up front with the other third after the successful hit. He made sure to mail the payments from locations totally removed from any he usually used.

Arranging for the hit had calmed him. His major problem was about to evaporate. He was ready to relax and celebrate. He decided to go out and enjoy an evening in New Orleans.

He found Ray and Jerry eager to drive the hour north into New Orleans. He knew that the two young body guards were a little stir crazy by being on the boat for so long. He had relaxed the rule about their drinking by allowing one drink per day and when one of them wanted to enjoy more than one the other one had to refrain and stay sober.

Ray and Jerry were upbeat about the trip to New Orleans. They would have liked to be able to enjoy a few drinks, but they knew that it was their job to stay sober and alert.

Had Remi known that his phone had been compromised he would not have been celebrating.

Kekoa alerted Brian of the assassination arrangements and suggested that they set up a fake mainland meeting in San Diego and set a trap for the assassin.

Brian asked how that would be arranged.

Kekoa said that he would send a tip to Remy from one of the folks that Remy had labeled "informer" on his phone. The tip was between Brian and his client. It would give a meeting location in the San Diego Balboa park at a bench located along a walking path where there were only three secluded spots for a sniper to stand and get a clear shot of whoever was sitting on the Bench. He made the point that it would be dangerous, but he had learned about a gun carrying drone from Johnnie that he would order and learn to operate.

When the time came for the assassination, he would go first to the bench location and be flying his drone like some individual out with his toy. Then when Brian came walking along, he would walk away from the bench and have his drone flying up to locate the assassin. He added that the best spot for someone to shoot a person sitting on the bench was a large maple tree surrounded by bushes standing on the hill in front of it. He hoped that the assassin would pick that spot. As he walked away from the bench, he would have his drone flying about as if he were learning to fly it but in fact, he would have it looking for the assassin to get into place and prepare to shoot.

Once he verified that person had a weapon, Kekoa said he would take him out before he could get a shot off.

Brian asked what the weather forecast for the coming week was in San Diego. He was relieved to learn that it would be warm and sunny. This would let him wear a hat that would conceal the fact that he was wearing his entire Kevlar outfit including his head protection since the weather allowed him to have on a large hat and wear sunglasses.

Kekoa said that he planned to have his suit on as well, but he would forgo the head gear. He wanted to look like an older person acting like a kid playing with his new toy.

Brian nodded and suggested that Kekoa be faster that Leilani had been on the last case when that assassin had been able to shoot him in the chest. He still had some aches from that time.

Kekoa laughed and said that he would be on the trigger-happy side versus trying to follow police procedure. He added that he planned to take three deadly shots and end it before anything began.

He put the meeting time and location tip into Remy's phone and then monitored it to see if there would be an outgoing call to the assassin. He was relieved to get confirmation of the call. He listened as the sniper responded that he was familiar with the park and would find the bench in question and be prepared for a quick shot and then a quick departure.

The sniper had no clue as to what would happen, but he was right about his quick departure.

Death Broker

A week later at Balboa Park, Kekoa walked casually along the walking path acting as if he were playing with his small drone as he approached the bench from one direction and Brian approached from the other direction. He had the drone flying high enough to see that someone was standing next to the tree at the top of the small hill in front of the bench. As Brian approached the bench he turned and began to walk away but he guided the drone into position to the back side of the tree.

As Brian was about to sit down, the assassin began to raise his rifle. Kekoa did not hesitate but flew the drone down behind the assassin and shouted as loud as he could.

The assassin must have heard the drone or Kekoa's clear shout and turned to look. He turned halfway around and Kekoa fired and shot him once through the left temple and once through the neck. The assassin fell over from the bullet impacts and landed on his right side.

He had indeed made a quick departure but not the one that he thought he would make.

Kekoa ran with his drone controller in hand up the small hill. Brian ran up the hill with his gun drawn. Neither the armed drone nor Brian's weapon was needed.

The assassin was dead.

Brian looked around to see if there were any observers. There were none. He suggested they leave immediately.

Kekoa removed the gun from the drone and put the drone away in a bag that he was carrying. He put the gun in the deep pocket on the side of his cargo pants.

They left everything untouched and slowly walked back to where they had left their rental car.

On the way, Kekoa put the gun into the trash barrel that was located at the end of the walk as the path got to the parking lot. He had used one of Remy's black-market guns and had carefully put Remi's finger prints on the bullets that he had loaded. He knew that Remi was out on his boat and would have a fool proof alibi for the shooting, but it would send a message to him that he should stay away from hiring assassins.

Once back to their car Brian drove to the airport and turned in the car. They then took the tram to the airport and walked to where their charter plane was located. Before takeoff, Kekoa used the informant's phone and sent a message to the local police letting them know of a shooting in the park and where they should look.

Kekoa knew that Remy would have a solid alibi because he was out on his yacht in the Gulf of Mexico but when the police contacted him, he would also know that his assassination scheme had been thwarted.

Remy was indeed out in the Gulf for the very reason that he wanted a solid alibi if his involvement in the assassination was at all suspected. He expected a call at any moment from the assassin that would let him know that O'Brien was dead.

When that call did not come in during the expected time, he began to worry.

The San Diego police did a solid investigation and found the gun in the trash container. The gun was clean of finger prints but it was only a few hours later when the finger prints on the bullets were found. One of Remy's old traffic violations had yielded the finger prints that were on the bullets.

The call from the San Diego police to his cell phone came only a day later while Remy was still out on his yacht. He had a solid alibi, but the police wanted to know how his finger prints had been on the bullets that were in an unregistered three-fifty-seven hand gun with a silencer that had killed a person also having an unregistered sniper's rifle. He let them know that he owned several small gun shops in the San Diego area and that maybe the bullets had been purchased there and he might have loaded the bullets while he visited the shop and helped some customer. He said perhaps the fact that the gun was not registered meant that it was a gun that the customer had come in with to buy bullets for. He said that he had no idea who the person that had been shot might be.

The fact that an unregistered gun that had bullets with his fingerprints on them had been used to kill the assassin raised the specter of a person that had a very detailed understanding of his business.

The fact that he had been able to get fingerprints with which to imprint the bullets put the entire situation on a level that Remi had never anticipated. It was beyond the simple and into the almost impossible.

He realized he was dealing with a person that was beyond just being good. He was dealing with a person that he now categorized as exceptional.

He now knew that he faced not only a very smart but also a very deadly adversary willing to act in a deadly way. He could not afford to underestimate him again. He needed to somehow get ready for a more formidable confrontation. A confrontation that he had to win. He decided that he was going to limit his travels and was going to arrange to have a small army of protectors living within a few minutes of his yacht. He felt that the yacht was in the safest location he could find.

On the flight back to Maui, Brian said that they needed to arrange to have Remy arrested before he figured out another way to try to eliminate either he or Kekoa.

Kekoa agreed and suggested that they monitor Remy's calls and locations and see about finalizing the information they needed to turn the case over to one to the three government agencies. He commented that it would be a relief to close the case even if they got zero reward out of it.

Brian agreed and suggested they put on the steam and accelerated in getting the case closed and turned over.

<u>Chapter 9: Turnover Prep</u>

Being back on Maui and being with the family made a huge difference for both Brian and Kekoa. They both took the time to enjoy their lunches and the dinners were especially fun since Anela was now a regular and Marvin and Bailey often joined them.

Annie felt the tension that the two had been showing slowly go out just as the tide went out each evening.

He and Kekoa worked for more than twelve hours a day for a solid week organizing the materials they had on Remi's gun shop business in the US. Kekoa organized the US into an East Coast, Middle of the country and West Coast businesses and set up the information in that fashion. Each file had store locations, managers names, local banks that were used, the percentage that was skimmed off and sent to a specific offshore bank, the offshore bank's location, account number, the account manager's name, and the amount of money in that bank.

It took them another week to separately organize the black-market gun smuggling business in a similar fashion. The significant difference was the amount of money in the Bangkok bank and the location of the banks from which the money came. It was a complex case of money coming from multiple countries via multiple banks. They figured that the IRS would have their hands full in trying to get that case organized into an iron clad one.

Another feature of the gun smuggling operation was that they had been able to identify the trucking companies that transported ninety percent of the guns across the border from the US to Mexico and the ones that moved the guns across the border to Canada. These trucking companies were owned by intermediate companies but eventually it all led back to Remi. This had been a difficult trail to follow but Kekoa's hacking ability proved invaluable. He was also able to identify the shipping companies used to move the guns to overseas markets. This information would be invaluable in seizing any weapons that were still in transit and it would enable the coast guard to seize the ships.

When they were done organizing the files that they would turn over, Brian contacted Joe Brown to get his guidance and advice on how to manage turning the case over.

Joe listened to the information that Brian was outlining. He gave a small whistle when the size of the case began to take shape in his mind. The dollar amounts were so unbelievable that he kept asking if the dollar amounts were accurate.

Brian reassured him that if anything the money amounts would most likely be higher.

Joe commented that not only was the case spread across multiple US IRS districts, but the gun smuggling part put the Homeland Security Investigation Unit and the Alcohol, Tabaco, and Firearms Unit into the mix as well. He added that he was not sure witch group would handle the Thailand connection, but he said that he was sure the IRS would want to investigate the tax angle associated with the money located there. He suggested that he set up one meeting to cover the US IRS portion of the case. A second session to cover the Thailand IRS portion of the case. And a third session to link in both HSI and ATF portions of the case.

He asked if Brian and Kekoa were flexible as to meeting times and dates.

Brian replied that they were flexible but that he would appreciate it if meetings could be scheduled in the middle of the week so that travel could be conveniently scheduled.

Joe agreed to make the meetings happened on one of the three middle days of the week.

Once he got off the phone, he called his boss to let her know what he had just learned about one of the largest tax evasion, money laundering schemes and gun smuggling operations that the agency had ever been involved in.

He asked her if she wanted to be involved in a series of meetings that would focus on getting the detailed information about the operation that then could be used to solidify the cases.

She declared that she wanted to be an integral part of it and that she would bring HSI and ATF onboard after they had the IRS sessions in hand.

He appreciated the fact that his boss immediately recognized the fact that two other US agencies would also need to get involved.

She asked who was bringing the case to them. She gave a small laugh and said that she had heard about Brian when she was promoted to her current position and the fact that his information already put three billionaires in prison. She was amazed when she learned that the case might be more than twenty billion dollars in size. She added that not only Brian's information put the billionaires in prison but the reward for doing so had made him a very wealthy person.

Joe let her know that Brian had turned over much of the reward to the victims that had been involved in those cases. He let her know that he was also aware of Brian's generous donations to several charities.

She volunteered to have her support call the appropriate IRS units together. She suggested four IRS sessions. Three to cover the US gun shop business. One to cover the Thailand bank account. Then they could hold the meetings with HSI and ATF.

She added that it would let the IRS get rolling immediately and it allowed her time to bring the leadership of the other two agencies on board before holding meetings with them. She added that this was a case that she wanted to have a lead position in.

Joe got agreement to have the meetings placed in the three middle days of the week and then thanked her for arranging the meetings.

He then called Brian back and let him know that there would be a minimum of five initial meetings where the case would be handed over to the IRS, and then a meeting with a combination team made up of the ATF and HSI.

Brian thanked him for ensuring a middle-of-the-week meeting timing and that he would be pleased to attend them.

He then shared the fact that he had thwarted one assassination attempt and suggested that the IRS be prepared to act as soon as possible to arrest Remi.

Joe asked if they could hold the West Coast meeting first. Then get the arrest warrant the next day for that string of gun shops. And after that plan and execute the arrest action on the next feasible day.

Brian agreed that would be a very good sequence. He suggested that Joe arrange for a large arresting team and any other support that was normal for the IRS when they would face a reluctant and potentially heavily armed group.

He added that once Remi was in custody, they could hold the rest of the meetings without the threat of having some sort of potential gun battle or some other type of personal retribution hanging over their heads.

After the call with Joe and getting things rolling, Brian shared the situation with Annie.

Annie shook her head and commented that he was indeed becoming a copy of Alex in action. She then asked why he had been reluctant to share the assassination attempt with her.

He smiled and said that he had wanted her paintings to continue to reflect the joy she seemed to be expressing in her latest paintings. He figured worrying about him might have a negative effect on the joy he saw in her paintings.

She gave him a hug and said that the joy she was expressing came from him and the girls. She was feeling a sense of freedom that she had never expected to feel again.

She asked how he had been able to dodge the linkage with the shooting at the San Diego Park and wondered if he was worried that it might come back to haunt him in the future.

Kekoa spoke up and said that it would be very unlikely since there was no weapon to trace since the local police had both the assassin's body, his weapon and the weapon that had killed him. It would be a cold case that eventually would be hanging like an albatross around Remi's neck.

Annie shook her head and said that the two of them were a deadly pair.

She then asked if any of the meetings would be held in Cincinnati.

Brian said that he was trying to get the one about the money held in the Bangkok bank to be held there and asked what she had in mind.

Annie shared the fact that she and Alex were trying to have a joint art show and a fund raiser. They had been talking about scheduling that at the Cincinnati River Front Park, having a band, refreshments and a large tent with her art show held under it.

The theme of the art show would be Scapes from around the US. The fund-raising theme would be "helping hands for those in need."

Kekoa asked what the Scapes theme meant.

Annie laughed and said that the term was a very painter centric term that captured the idea of seascapes, landscapes, cityscapes. Any of these scapes would be accepted in the art show. She had enough of her own scape paintings to make the showing worthwhile, but she wanted to open the showing to as wide a variety of artists and scapes as possible.

Brian asked if a meeting held toward the end of July would work and added that the O'Neil and Ikaika team would come up with a good donation to Alex's cause and maybe even buy some of the scape paintings that would be shown.

Annie said that the timing was sufficiently out in the future that it would work. If he gave her the date, she would work with Alex to get things planned, organized, and advertised. She smiled and added that all money going to either cause would be greatly appreciated but that she did not want Brian paying for her paintings as much as he had paid for the first paint of hers that he had purchase.

Linda spoke up and asked if she and Laurie could be the ones to arrange the entertainment. They shared the fact that they had scheduled in the entertainment for the coming weekends pool side party to celebrate Kekoa's and Anela's engagement.

They figured that if that went well, they could do the next one for the Cincinnati event. They said that they had several friends there that were trying get a start with their bands.

Annie agreed that was a good idea but stipulated that they had to agree to schedule in a professional headlining band and that they should limit the opening bands to two.

Linda and Laurie readily agreed and said they would contact their friends to get them to identify some new upcoming groups and a headliner that was currently popular.

Kekoa then went out to the veranda and examined the material they planned to turn over.

He suggested an overall visual of the entire operation that featured each of the US's three sections and total dollar value on a large map. He suggested that a map would have the greatest impact if it were a large physical map that had each of the operations highlighted and the flow of the skimmed money flowing to the offshore banks.

Brian agreed that the map was a great way of giving an overall view and that the way the files were organized would solidify the case for all concerned. He pointed out that it would need to be a world map.

They had just agreed on a world map when Annie volunteered to have her art group produce a world map painting for them.

Brian said that would be a great way to get the large world map produced. He added that she and the girls would have to be the ones that added the detail that was confidential.

He had been working on a family surprise. That afternoon he called Kaia and asked if she was OK with him coming up for a surprise visit and offered to bring dinner. Kaia said that he was welcome, but she wanted to prepare the dinner. Once he was off the phone, he asked Annie if she would like to come along.

It turned out that Annie, Linda, and Laurie were all eager to go up to Pukalani, "the window to heaven" where Brian had grown up. It had been several weeks since their last visit and they all enjoyed going there.

The reason for his visit was to turn over a trust fund to Kaia and Koni, the two people he considered as his mother and father. The trust would provide them with a substantial yearly income for the rest of their lives.

On the way Annie asked him if the visit was some sort of special event.

Brian nodded in the affirmative.

Annie suggested that they get Kaia a bouquet, a bottle of her favorite wine and Koni a case of his favorite Island beer.

Brian thanked her for thinking about the personal touch and made the stops to get what she had suggested.

The drive up to Pukalani brought back memories of his school bus rides and later of driving his old car, that he still used, back and forth to school and to his first job as a fast-food store clerk.

He stopped halfway up the drive and got out to enjoy the view of Lanai, Kaho'olawe, and the Molokini Crater. He pointed to the windmills on Kealaloloa Ridge and commented that they went up when he was away in Ireland in college.

Annie commented that she had a painting of this view that she was going to show in her upcoming art show.

They finished the drive up to the parking area and all got out.

Annie held up a single red rose and said that it was for his birth mother and took Brian's hand and walked out to where her ashes were buried and put the rose on the small stone that commemorated the spot. She caught the tears in the corner of Brian's eyes and knew that she had done the right thing.

They then all went into the house through the kitchen door and were pleasantly greeted by the aroma of roast chicken and a variety of yet to be discovered parts of the dinner.

Linda had the bouquet of flowers and Laurie had the bottle of wine that they eagerly presented to Kaia.

A few moments later Koni arrived, and Brian presented him with the case of his favorite beer.

Kaia suggested they get the table set and enjoy her baked Huli, Huli chicken with Hawaiian asparagus and a Hawaiian baked potato that featured chopped ham, bacon, bell peppers and onions all smothered under a layer of cheese soup.

Annie commented that she was surprised at the elaborate dinner offering.

Once everyone was seated Kaia looked at Brian and commented that the last time he had asked to visit, he had introduced Annie. She was wondering what he had in mind this time.

Brian smiled and complemented her on the great chicken and the out of this world baked potato. He added that this time he did not have as great of a surprise as when he had introduced Annie, but he did have a surprise that he hoped would allow she and Koni to spend the rest of their lives in comfort and doing the things they wanted to do. He said that he especially wanted them to travel wherever they desired and not worry about money. He pulled out a folder that he placed on the table and said that it contained the paper work for a trust that would give them at least ten times the income that they currently generated. He added that the two were its trustees and controlled the trust.

Kaia looked over to Annie and asked if she had known about the surprise.

Annie shook her head and replied that this was the first time that she had known about the surprise, but she was certainly pleased with Brian's generosity.

Koni commented that the gift he was being given was a relief in the sense that he and Kaia could now manage Pukalani together and not worry about their finances. It would allow him to join full time in giving back to the Islands what they had given to him.

He asked if it put Brian in any cash flow issues.

Brian shook his head and commented that he was in the process of trying to give back to the world around him the immense amount of money that had miraculously come his way. He added that the money was flowing in faster than he knew what to do with it.

After a desert of brown sugar grilled pineapple with a scoop of passion fruit ice cream on top of it, Annie shared the fact that she was putting on an art show in Cincinnati and everyone was invited. However, if Kaia and Koni were planning to go, they should plan to fly on the charter plane that Brian now had exclusive use of.

Koni lifted his glass and gave a toast to Brian, "the son that wouldn't let me carry his luggage and now won't let me fly commercially."

<u>Chapter 10: The Warrant</u>

The Gulf was calm, and the water was reflecting the rays of the early morning eastern sun rise. Remi was sitting out on the deck enjoying a breakfast of two poached eggs, a piece of toast smothered in strawberry jam and a steaming cup of coffee. He was enjoying the early morning but emotionally disturbed by his situation. He felt like he did not have control of his destiny. He felt like a coon being chased by baying hounds in the middle of the night and that his yacht had become the tree he was hiding in as he tried to be invisible to those hounds.

The yacht was now fully staffed with a crew of ten heavily armed guards, a chef, a boat captain and his two personal bodyguards. He had ten more armed guards back at the dock where he moored his boat. When the boat was at the dock five armed guards were on duty around the clock. Only he, his two body guards, the Chef and the captain lived on board. The Chef had been given the choice of staying on board or at the local hotel. He had chosen to stay on board.

Remi felt most relaxed when he was out on the yacht enjoying the Gulf waters. The coordination of managing the situation meant that most evenings found the yacht tied to the pier. This allowed the guards to get a normal night's sleep and allowed the time required to get the yacht fueled and serviced.

He wanted to change the situation. He was pondering the situation. He wondered why he had retreated so far from waging a head-long battle with whomever was determined to bring him down. He continued to ponder the fact that he did not know who had hired O'Neill and therefore who he needed to attack. That meant that other than a very capable young lawyer, he had no target to eliminate and his try to eliminate O'Neill had been a monumental failure.

He needed a breakthrough in finding out who was after him and he did not see that happening any time soon.

His network of informants had found no link to anyone in the gunrunning business or any of his US competitors. He did not have a clue where to look next. He felt that he was in an information desert. He was looking for that oasis where he would find the person he was looking for. He needed to find the path up the mountain that led to the cross-legged guru who would know the who and the why. He concluded that he needed a miracle.

As he watched the guards, five to a side with their weapons at their feet, take up their idle time fishing, he felt more like he was sitting on a charter fishing boat than on one of the most luxurious yachts in the world.

He wanted to feel in control and that was so far from reality that he tried to focus on his breakfast.

He cursed the current situation and thought about alternative ways to spend his time. The idea of flying around the world on a private plane and visiting all the famous sites came to mind and he decided to arrange that. That would make it hard for anyone to take personal action against him, but it would not do anything that would help him take a counter action against his invisible adversary.

He sopped up the remains of the poached eggs with a buttery piece of toast. He had his coffee refilled and sat back and watched the sun go behind what seemed to be the only cloud in the morning sky. It seemed a message being sent to him about his situation. "Your life is behind a cloud."

At the same time Remy was pondering his future, Brian and Kekoa were landing in San Diego where they would attend the first meeting where they were to meet with the IRS West Coast team. Once they landed, they watched as a long tube was maneuvered out of the plane to the waiting van.

Marvin put the tube on the top of his van and asked what they were carrying in it.

Brian let him know it was a world map with an amazing story documented on it and that Marvin had been a part of most of what was on the map.

Marvin asked if he would be allowed to see the map.

Brian said he would arrange a quick look for him.

The stand for the map came in a series of small cardboard tubes and boxes. The whole assembly would take some time to assemble. They had called ahead and arranged for a team to assemble the stand and put up the map that had been done on canvas.

The map turned out to be ten feet high and twenty-four feet long. The two of them had hired a group of Annie's art students to paint the map and then Annie, Linda and Laurie had put on the gun shops and all the other confidential details. Each gun shop location had a little map key box that gave the details about their cash flow that was also available in the reports. In fact, the map represented everything that was presented in all the individual the reports. It was the clearest depiction that one could display in a holistic depiction.

The two girls said they were very happy to have earned a great chunk of their college money and said that they would love to provide such services often.

Annie laughed and had told them not to get too greedy.

Brian and Kekoa had been impressed with the map and said that they figured those viewing the map would thank them for having made the operation seem very simple and straight forward. They were sure that any jury would be able to grasp the situation immediately. They were eager to display the map and tell the story that it visually depicted.

Joe Brown and several of his Cincinnati team met them at the San Diego IRS office building and the crew to assemble the stand and put up the map were also with him. They carried everything inside. He guided them to a large meeting room where a host of people were sitting around a large meeting table. He introduced his boss, Madiline, the West Coast IRS leader, Matt, the center of the country leader Ileza, and the East coast leader, Jeffery.

He said that the meeting had expanded because they had all wanted to be present during this first session. He added that he hoped Brian and Kekoa were OK with the larger meeting.

The meeting was not until the following morning, but Madiline had suggested getting started with introductions and that evening to have a dinner that would give them all a chance to meet each other. He made the point that it was his first time to meet the leaders of the three regions.

Brian thanked them all for coming. He briefly gave them his back ground and his focus on finding wayward billionaires. He then introduced Kekoa as the chief reason that the IRS, the ATF and the HSI would get the detailed information that would provide a road map to solid court cases.

He added that he and Kekoa had come prepared to hand over the material to everyone present and doing so this afternoon would make it much easier on the two of them since it would reduce the weight of the luggage that they had brought with them. He smiled and added that it might even reduce the number of turnover meetings that would be needed and speed up the gathering of the detailed information that the IRS would need to do to get the cases to court.

He asked Joe to send a team out with a couple of heavy-duty dollies to bring in the boxes holding the documents.

He sat down and asked if there were any questions.

Madiline asked why he had selected billionaires as targets.

Brian smiled and said that the kernel of that focus had been planted when he was a young boy and watched a person with a very expensive suit take a bill, probably a dollar, from a beggar's donation box.

That had caused him to begin watching the behavior of well to do people. Many of them were visitors to Maui that seemed to be spoiled well to do persons that seemed insensitive to the situations of the people around them. From there as he grew older, he became sensitized to the apparent snobbery of the well to do. During his college years he slowly came to focus on the top of the wealth ladder, billionaires. The fact that they seemed to pay the least amount of taxes versus their income triggered his desire to verify that they were not cheating.

He was disappointed to find that they were coddled by very favorable tax laws that allowed them to pay proportionally less taxes than all the hard-working common people.

Then a news item featuring what seemed an outright illegal trickster-like maneuver of legally stealing a Black person's hard-earned ownership of a hotel building sealed his focus. He smiled and added that specific billionaire was now serving more than twenty years in jail and that the IRS had fined him multi-millions of dollars. The properties stolen by that billionaire, as well as the money the people who had been cheated would have earned over the years was now in the hands of the victims.

The boxes with the turnover reports arrived and Joe took the time to have them opened and the files handed to each specific regional IRS leader.

Madiline looked at the pile put in front of her and commented that she had not come prepared to carry that amount of material home with her.

Kekoa commented that he had the method that would allow her to easily take all home. He got up and handed her a thumb drive and said that everything in the files in front of her was on the drive including all the material in all the files.

He then walked around and handed each of the other leaders a thumb drive.

Joe commented that the physical pile files and binders in front of her would be sent to Cincinnati and be available in his office.

There was silence around the table as each of the IRS leaders took in the material in front of them and briefly thumbed through the files.

One of them asked how long the two of them had been gathering the information.

Kekoa replied that it had been almost four years. He added that the gun running had added almost two years to the case. But all of it had required a huge amount of online and in the field work. He added that he had been the lucky one since he was the IT hack that sat leisurely on a veranda in Maui that overlooked the ocean while Brian had the hard work of being the one out in the field doing the field verification.

Someone else asked how they had been able to pay for the expenses associated with gathering all the material.

Brian smiled and said that the generosity of the IRS from the previous cases had easily covered the significant expense associated in documenting this case. He added that he was prepared to extend that generosity by paying for that evening's meal. He added that he had been conscientious about his spending when he was out in the field, but he had not skimped. He had arranged that period so that his home life was minimally affected.

Madiline smiled and said that she would accept his offer to pay for the evening outing and that she was ready to call it a day so she could spend a couple of hours with Joe to review the material that had been turned over. She asked if he and Kekoa would be available at the end of the meeting on the following day to for additional questions.

She added that she had arranged with the judge to issue a warrant based on his seeing and understanding the information associated with the case.

Brian said that he was sure that the map that she would see in the morning would be the key piece that would convince the judge to issue an arrest warrant. He added that the map was a true piece of art that was painted by the world-renowned professional artist, Annie Scotts, and her team of artists.

Madiline shook her head and said he must be kidding; she owned a forest scene by that artist. She asked how he had been able to have her paint a map for him?

He smiled and said because she volunteered to do so and added that she was his significant other.

"Wow, I can't wait until dinner. I will want to hear more about how the two of you met," Madiline commented.

Kekoa and he left and checked into their hotel.

That evening both Kekoa and he were overwhelmed by the multitude of questions that were asked. By the time the evening ended the two of them were exhausted.

That evening back at the hotel on the elevator going up to their two suites, Brian commented that he now knew how a sponge felt when it was being squeezed dry.

Kekoa said that he was going to take a hot shower and hit the hay. He needed all the sleep he could get.

Early the next morning before the meeting was to start, Joe, Brian and Kekoa entered the meeting room. They looked at the huge world map that took up the entire wall at the end of the room.

Joe commented that it was truly a work of art. He walked slowly from one end to the other. He said that he had spent several hours the previous evening flipping through the files, but the map made it so simple that he wished he had just gone to sleep instead of burning the midnight oil.

Madiline was the next person to enter. She went to the corner of the map and took note of all the signatures of the artists that had helped paint the world map. She noted that there were three Scotts signatures. She said that she did not know that Annie had two daughters.

Brian smiled and said that he had been three times lucky and had gotten all three as a gift from above.

By that time almost all the other leaders had arrived and were all standing at and taking in the information not only of their section of the map but browsing through the rest. Without exception they all commented on how the map made a very complicated case seem surprisingly simple.

Joe called the meeting to order. He said that he would like to have each regional leader stand at the map and explain to the rest of them what they understood about their portion of the case and how they would approach getting that section ready to present to a judge and jury.

They would start on the West Coast, then review the East Coast and then the center of the country. Each area leader should state what kind of help they needed from Kekoa or Brian.

He said that by that time it would most likely be lunch time.

After lunch, his team would explain how they were thinking about handling the Bangkok gunrunning account.

By late afternoon, the group was exhausted but it was clear that the case, though overwhelmingly large, was now well understood by every member in the room.

Madiline shared the fact that she had convinced the judge to come to their meeting. The goal was to get him to issue an arrest warrant. She asked that each team, beginning with the Bangkok team, then the East Coast team, followed by the Mississippi team give him a five-minute presentation of their cases. Then the West Coast team would close with their case and the amount of a tax dodge that the total case represented.

She asked if everyone was ready. After getting the affirmative from everyone in the meeting she called the judge.

When the judge arrived, she gave him a brief overview from Bangkok to the Eastern Seaboard and then took him across to the West Coast.

Then he listened as each area leader took him through the same walk across the map and explained their portion.

The judge shook his head and commented on the ease of understanding such a complicated case. He said his only question was whether all the documentation would be available by the time the case came to court.

Madiline assured him that each case would be fully documented before it came in front of any of the judges and juries that would hear the cases and that he would be the first of the cases and set the tone for the remainder of the trials.

The judge said she would have the arrest warrant before the end of the day. He commented that he wanted the map to be in his court when the case was presented.

After the judge left, Joe said that there was one last item that needed to be discussed and that was the staffing of the arresting team and the timing of the arrest. He suggested that each team leader volunteer five members and that Madiline assign another ten IRS folks to be part of an arresting team.

Madiline asked why he was suggesting such a large arresting team.

Brian shared the fact that Kekoa had information that Remi had hired a total of twenty professional gun toting guards and that the rest of the team around Remi were professional gun men as well.

Madiline shook her head and said that Brian had not only brought one of the largest cases to the IRS but apparently one of the more dangerous ones. She was quiet for a moment. She asked where the arrest was likely to be made.

Kekoa replied that currently Remi seemed to be staying on his yacht at the very southern tip of Louisiana.

Madiline nodded and said that she would get the additional personnel assigned and that she was adding at least one helicopter to the arresting squad.

She said that as soon as all that was arranged, they would make the arrest.

<u>Chapter 11: The Arrest</u>

The meeting ended when the arrest warrant was brought in.

It was clear that Madiline was fully supportive but concerned about the upcoming confrontation that might happen during the arrest.

The arrest of Remi was scheduled to take place two weeks out. He and Kekoa discussed the situation as they flew back to Maui. They agreed that a convoy of IRS cars driving down highway seven to the marina where Reni moored his yacht might give away the arrest action and permit Remi to flee or it might make the action a very dangerous confrontation.

Brian suggested they arrange to rent five speed boats from the marina close to where the yacht was moored to be used to shadow the yacht if it chose to leave the pier before the arrest could be made. Plexiglass shields could be installed on those boats to protect the IRS officers in them. These officers could pretend to be a group of kayakers. They could arrive in a variety of older cars carrying kayaks.

The arresting officers would be the boaters that would shadow the yacht and the additional officers in that group could then proceed on foot to be part of the IRS contingent that would be at the pier.

Kekoa added that the mobile command and communication van should remain just outside of New Orleans and any of the assigned helicopters would provide visual linkage to where the yacht was moored or located out on the Gulf if it moved.

Brian added that the two of them should drive down early on the morning of the arrest and get themselves ready to participate. He suggested they each get a hooded wind breaker that had the large letters, IRS, emblazoned in white across the back and that they wear their full Kevlar suits including the head gear.

Kekoa asked if they should make sure that all the IRS agents also had the full body Kevlar suits.

Brian nodded and agreed that would be a good idea and possibly save lives.

He then asked if there was a way to find out the types of weapons that Remi's guards would be using.

Kekoa replied that he could get a good idea how they were armed via the boat cameras that he had access to. He later spent time to get an inventory of the weapons. Two thirds of the guards were armed with AR-15's and the remainder had what appeared to be shot guns.

After landing in Maui, Brian called Joe and shared what he and Kekoa had discussed. He learned that the agents did not have Kevlar suits and Joe agreed that would be a good idea. He agreed with holding the communication and control center just outside of New Orleans and with how to get the number of agents close to the yacht. He said he would arrange for managing the coordination.

He took Brian up on the offer to supply the Kevlar suits and said he would send back the sizes for the people that would participate.

Over breakfast with Annie and the girls, Brian shared the very positive feedback the world map had received. He added that everyone involved in its creation should get a letter of recognition and a one-thousand-dollar check for having participated in drawing the map.

Annie said that would make her art students very happy. She added that she would hold a special celebration to present them with the checks. She thanked him for being so generous.

She then asked if the US Coast Guard should be involved just in case the yacht seemed to be making a successful sea get away.

Brian nodded and agreed that was a good idea and he would pass it on to the Joe and Madiline.

Far away Remi was sitting on the deck of his yacht wondering how to get on with his life and forget about whomever was poking their nose into his business.

He had unsuccessfully tried to get rid of the intermediary O'Brian. He thought of it as an expensive and miserable failure. He had his entire network looking for the person that seemed to be so interested in his business and so far, that network had come up dry.

He decided to take on enough fuel to travel to the southern part of Brazil without having to stop. He arranged for a mooring spot at Guaruja. He figured it would give him a chance to travel around Brazil and enjoy himself. It would also put him far enough off his normal routine that anyone following would stand out like a sore thumb and he would finally find out who that person was.

The captain suggested storing the extra fuel that was required to make the trip non-stop along the front rail of the sun deck. He had the fifty-gallon fuel drums lined two layers deep and covered by a white tarp. He had immediately made smoking on the front deck off limits.

Remi thought extra fuel made his yacht look more like a cargo ship than he cared to think about. He decided that since it was the only way to make the trip without stopping, he would just ignore the situation.

Now it was only a matter of time as he waited to get a visa from Brazil. He had paid extra to expedited getting it issued and he hoped to get it in the next couple of days. He was anxious to get underway.

Joe and Madiline worked through the details of making the arrest and were following most of Brian's suggestions. Madiline commented that Brian made the execution of the arrest action seem to be foolproof. She especially appreciated his concern for the safety of everyone involved as demonstrated by his willingness to foot the cost of the Kevlar outfits for everyone.

Joe commented that so far, the case materials that Brian had turned over gave the lawyers the winning hand.

He added that Brian had requested to be part of the arresting team.

Madiline asked if he was licensed to carry a weapon.

Joe laughed and said that he knew one person in Cincinnati that had put six bullets in a firing range bull's eye with a blind fold on and later he heard that Brian had duplicated her demonstration of skill. He shared the fact that the last billionaire that had tried to have him assassinated failed and that while bringing her in he had single handedly killed more than six of her hired guns.

Madiline said that was a side of Brian she had not envisioned as she talked with him. He seemed so kind and considerate that she would never have imagined him engaging in a gun fight.

Joe chuckled and commented that it was seldom a gun fight. It was Brian doing the shooting and the bad guys going down like ninepins.

He added that Brian had requested that he and Kekoa be allowed to wear an IRS wind breaker with large white IRS lettering across the back so the two of them would not be mistaken for adversaries.

Madiline nodded said that would be acceptable.

She went over all the details and added that the two helicopters would have two snipers and the Coast Guard would send out one of their ships from the Houston area and be available if needed.

Joe said that it seemed that it was time to get on with making the arrest.

Madiline said she would send out a message calling for everyone to meet in New Orleans to get organized and to do a dry run of what they would do.

The week of the arrest, the entire team gathered outside of New Orleans to simulate how they would all be involved and what their actions would be.

Kekoa suggested they all wear the entire Kevlar body suit and the head gear, ball caps and sunglasses. He pointed to the plexiglass shields that would be placed in the boats and said that each speed boat should only carry two people and they should stand under the top angled piece and shoot through the hole provided and if they were not shooting, they should slide the cover over the hole shut. He made the point that the shields had sides so the boat could maneuver and the two people on board would be protected.

Brian walked around and checked out the participants. He found two that he suspected were not wearing the Kevlar suits. One was a petite young female agent and the other person seemed to be with her and perhaps her boyfriend. He asked each of them how their bullet proof protection felt.

They both said that if felt perfect.

He suspected them of lying. He suggested that they be part of a demonstration on how effective the vests were by letting him shoot each of them in the chest with his pellet gun.

Silence seemed to sweep across the gathering like the dark before a storm. Everyone stopped what they were doing, and silence swept across the area like a fog sweeping in from the sea. The all were looking to see what would happen.

Madiline came over and asked the two to show her their Kevlar vests.

Both said that they had not worn them for the practice.

Madiline told them they had ten minutes to get them on or they would be fired for disobeying her directive. The two ran off in the direction of the hotel.

She looked at Brian and asked him if he would have shot them with his pellet gun.

Brian chuckled and said he didn't own a pellet gun.

Madiline chuckled and thanked him for spotting the two and making them a good example of what not to do. She walked away with the feeling of confidence in having followed Brian's advice on how to make the arrest.

The sun seemed to break through the clouds and the tension embracing the group seemed to release like the hot air from the top hole of a balloon. The entire gathering broke into laughter.

After a laugh, Madiline thanked him for taking the time to make sure the safety measures they had agreed on were being followed.

Brian nodded and let everyone know that he had a bad premonition about the upcoming arrest, and they should all watch each other's backs.

Joe had been watching all the IRS participants and he felt that Brian's actions and Kekoa's suggestions had clearly put them in lead positions with the IRS team and that they would all follow their suggestions.

The next day was "arrest" day. Joe suggested they all get a good night's rest and that early the following morning they would all make an early morning trip down highway seven to where Remy had his yacht.

Brian let him know that Kekoa and he were going down and spent the night on the beach. They were being driven down by Marvin, their van driver and for this trip he was their surfing buddy. They walked Joe over to the van and gave him a view of the interior.

Madiline had followed and commented that it was clear that they would have a tough night. She asked if they were up to having dinner with her and Joe at a traditional New Orleans restaurant for Jambalaya followed by a café au lait paired with a beignet.

Brian replied that he would love to do that, but he had Bananas Foster as his dessert on his mind.

The dinner was delightful, the food and dessert earned the reputation that drew people from around the world to New Orleans. Everyone commented on the great dinner.

Brian and Kekoa got into their van and headed south.

The sun was slowly sinking in the west as they drove down to where Remi had his yacht.

Brian said that he would like to verify that the yacht was moored where they expected it to be.

Marvin drove past the dock area and stopped the van to let Brian and Kekoa get out.

As Brian walked toward the dock it was clear that preparations to depart seemed to be underway.

He called Joe and let him know that the IRS team needed to move immediately because it appeared that Remi had decided to depart the area.

He and Kekoa were still in full Kevlar gear. They returned at a trot to the van and got their head gear, IRS vests and let Marvin know that they were planning to get on the yacht if possible.

They both were fully armed and took as much ammo with them as possible.

Marvin asked if they were sure they wanted to do it alone.

Brian said that he did not, but he was going to do it, nonetheless.

When they returned to the dock, they witnessed the mooring lines being pulled in.

They waited until the last possible moment then the ran as fast as they could to catch up to the yacht as it was pulling away.

Brian was the first to jump onto the very back. He turned and caught Kekoa by the wrist and helped him get on board. There was an area that had a tarp covering what they found out were large trash containers. They situated themselves behind the containers and sat quietly. Brian texted his thoughts to Kekoa that they should wait until morning and hope that the rest of the IRS team would catch up to the yacht.

Kekoa acknowledged by returning a green check mark.

Brian then texted Joe, let him know that he and Kekoa were on board the yacht. He told Joe to track his phone so he would know where to send the five speed boats but to make sure that no one called either his or Kekoa's phone.

Joe's first reaction was to text asking if he and Kekoa had a death wish. Then he responded that his team would be in place in less than forty-five minutes and that he had notified the Coast Guard, and their cutter would be making top speed from Huston to support them.

Madiline's reaction was to curse and ask whether Brian had gone crazy. She immediately got the two helicopters into the air and on their way. She then said that she was taking the command center van straight down to the pier and operate from there. She also suggested they put extra personnel in each of the five speed boats. She was now very concerned about Brian and Kekoa's safety and how the arrest plans seemed to have unraveled.

Remi felt a sense of relief as the boat made its way out into the Gulf. It felt like a weight was being lifted from his chest. His preparation seemed to be paying off. He had a small army of twenty protectors and soon he would be in international waters. He was going to enjoy a quiet night. He figured that in the morning he would watch the sunrise, enjoy a large breakfast, and then try his hand at fishing. There would be no hurry so the yacht could take on a slow cruising speed that would allow him to fish and it would also save on fuel usage. He knew that his decision to immediately leave the US was the right one.

For Brian and Kekoa the night seemed to pass as slow as cold molasses on a blustery snow blowing winter's day. They took turns sleeping. Both were wide awake when early in the morning they heard the whir of helicopters. They looked out and, in the distance, saw the five speed boats coming toward them.

Brian texted Kekoa to take the right walkway and he would take the left one. He texted that he expected the shooting to start as soon as the helicopters were spotted.

Remi had just put the first bite of his syrup covered pancake in his mouth when he heard a helicopter. He went to the side of the boat and looked back toward where he heard the sound and immediately instructed the captain to get them past the twelve-mile limit. He cursed and put down his fork and took out his weapon.

He then rousted a bunch of sleepy gunmen and told them to shoot the helios down. Several of them began shooting long before the copters were within range. It was clear to him that he had a bunch of gunmen that had never face what they were about to face.

The gunners in the helicopters had the range to return the fire and did so.

Brian stood up and shined his flashlight on the IRS on his back.

The firing coming in stopped as the two copters came in closer.

The speed boats were making great time and were rapidly closing in, but Bryan could feel the yacht surging forward.

After a brief exchange of gunfire down his side of the walk way he signaled Kekoa of his intention and climbed the ladder up to the con area. He entered the con with his gun drawn and instructed the captain to shut the engine down. He saw the captain reaching for his weapon.

Brian step in close and put his weapon to the captain's temple and said two and that at three he gun would fire.

The captain took his hand off the gun and throttled the yacht to idle.

Suddenly the exchange of gunfire with the helicopters reached a high crescendo. And it became clear that the speedboats had arrived and were having a heavy exchange with those on board.

Remi had not expected such an intense exchange and was huddling back into the kitchen area trying to keep from getting killed. He had no idea why the captain had come to an almost complete stop. He was contemplating going up to the con to find out when one of the gasoline barrels blew up and engulfed the entire front of the yacht in flames. He was thrown backwards and skidded across the deck and hit the bar. He sat for a moment in a stunned stupor.

A second barrel blew up and he was sure that the rest would soon follow.

He watched as several of his gunners who were in flames jumped over the side. The gunfire was now almost continuous. He stood up and looked around trying to decide what to do when a third gas drum blew up and knocked him against the bulkhead. He figured that it was time for him to abandon ship. He threw the life raft over the side and watched as it seemed to explode and then have the sides fill with air.

He jumped after it hoping to land in it. He hit the raft almost dead center, but he came in feet first and went right straight through the floor of the raft. He knew immediately that he was a dead man. He clawed his way to the surface, but he did not know how to swim and went down a second time.

From the con, Brian observed what had happened to Remi. He reached over and switched off the yacht's engines and took the keys with him. He had just reached the door leading out of the con when he was hit in the back. He turned and shot the captain through his forehead. He had not expected the captain to have a second gun. Luckily, it was a small caliber derringer. That oversight was going to cause him some pain, but it cost the captain his life. He stepped out and jumped down where Remi seemed to be going down for the last time.

Brian caught Remi by the back of his collar and pulled him to the surface. He was having a hard time as his Kevlar suit absorbed water. He struggled to pull Remi toward the raft and realized that the raft was slowly being blown away from him. He was about to let go of Remi when a splash hit near the raft and when that person came up out of the water, he realized it was Kekoa.

Kekoa pushed the raft toward him and Remi and then he got into the raft and reached out.

Brian grabbed Kekoa's arm and pushed Remi to him. Then he got in and helped pull a passed-out Remi on board.

After they had drained the water out of Remi he began to cough and come back to life.

Kekoa chuckled and said he was glad he did not need to do mouth to mouth resuscitation.

Brian looked around at the scene around the raft. The Coast Guard cutter had a stream of water hitting the remaining gasoline barrels and they had several lifeboats rescuing the men that had abandoned the yacht. Up in the sky he saw one helicopter that was trailing smoke that had turned and was heading back toward the beach, but the other was circling slowly. They came over the raft and lowered a basket.

Kekoa and he strapped Remi into the basket and watched as it was pulled up. Once he was up and secured the copter followed the first one toward the beach.

Brian gave them a salute and got a wiggle in return.

Brian sat down, looked at Kekoa and asked if he had been hit.

Kekoa put up three fingers and asked the same question and laughed when Brian put up his little finger. He asked what that meant.

Brian commented that it was a small caliber gun.

Chapter 12: Aftermath

Brian and Kekoa remained in the life raft for almost an hour as the men in the water were rescued and taken to the cutter. They had a ring side seat as the fire on the yacht was put out and all the remaining gas barrels were sprayed down to cool them off. They watched a contingent of Coast Guard personnel board the yacht. Then a coast guard rescue boat came by to pick them up.

Brian wanted to laugh when one of the first things he was asked was whether he had the keys to the yacht. He had forgotten them, but it turned out they were still in his pocket. He handed them over and watched as the sailor waved them in the air. The rescue boat went in and handed the keys to a sailor on the yacht and afterwards took the two of them to the coast guard cutter.

He and Kekoa were asked if they had shot anyone, and they both replied that they had. They were asked for their weapons which they put into an evidence bags that one of the sailors was holding.

They were then checked over by a corpsman who noted where they had been hit. He asked who had shot Brian in the back.

Brian replied that he was the captain of the yacht, and he was now dead.

The corpsman looked over at Kekoa and asked him about his bruises.

Kekoa shook his head and replied that he had been hit during an exchange of gun fire and had no idea who had shot him.

The yacht was put into tow, and the cutter proceeded slowly back toward shore.

Bryan and Kekoa were escorted to the con where they were introduced to the Coast Guard Cutter's Captain.

He asked if they were responsible for the destruction of a small army of killers.

Bryan shook his head and replied that he and Kekoa had only slowed things down so that everyone coming in support could get there to save the two of them. They had even abandoned the yacht to escape.

That brought a smile out on the Captain's face as he replied that putting a huge yacht on fire to slow things down was certainly an innovative way to do it. And jumping off to rescue a drowning person was certainly the act of two helpless people.

He then said that he had been instructed to anchor out but to send the two of them in by boat to the pier where the yacht had been moored.

It was a fast ride but to Brian, who was replaying what had just transpired, it seemed to be of a boat going through cold molasses. As they arrived, the entire contingent of IRS personnel were standing along the pier and gave a cheer when they stepped out of the boat onto the pier.

Madiline came forward and thanked the two for having made the capture and arrest of Remi possible. She added that she and Joe had both watched as Bryan opened the door of the con, pulled his gun, and shot someone inside and then jumped down into the water and saved Remi. They then watched as Kekoa jumped after him to help get Remi and he into the life raft. She commented that the two of them certainly had each other's backs. She added that several agents in the chase speed boats had been hit during the exchange of gun fire, but the Kevlar suits saved them. They would have some nasty bruises, but they now swore that they would never go into action again without their Kevlar vests.

Brian and Kekoa both handed her their IRS jackets and thanked her for the loan.

She laughed when she saw that they were handing them back with fingers through the holes where they had been shot. She said that the snipers in the helicopters had commented that the lettering helped them stay focused on the other shooters and taking out the ones threatening the two IRS people on the boat.

As they talked Madiline had been slowly walking them back up the pier. The agents that lined the pier had all been thanking Bryan and Kekoa and patting them on the back. It was clear that they were being greeted as conquering heroes returning from the war.

When they got to the end of the pier, Marvin was waiting for them with the van doors open. He welcomed them back and said that he would be happy to drive them to wherever they wanted to go.

Kekoa spoke up and said that going to get something to eat was number one on his list. He felt like an empty stomach ready to devour itself.

Joe said there was a small dinner used by folks working in the area that offered a basic menu. He asked if he could join in so they could discuss the actions that he needed the two to take so that the IRS could totally take over.

During what would have been considered a brunch, Joe shared the fact that the IRS legal team was recommending the seizure of all of Remi's physical properties such as his homes, boats, and the entire amount of money in the Bangkok account. They said that only the San Diego home would remain Remi's but the yacht he had there would be confiscated. He then informed Brian that when Remi had jumped over board and he had shot the captain, he technically, though inadvertently became the owner of the yacht because it crossed into international waters before he himself had jumped to save Remi.

Joe smiled and asked what Brian wanted to do with his new, slightly damaged yacht.

Brian shook his head and said that Remi's arrest was taking on a very different aura. He had envisioned watching the IRS put handcuffs on Remi and marching him down the pier. The actual events that had transpired in the last twenty-four hours was a bolt out of the blue. It was even more surprising than the gun battle and the repeated gas barrel explosions. He looked over at Kekoa and asked whether they should get the yacht repaired and have it taken to Maui where they could put it into service.

Kekoa smiled and said that he would like to enjoy it without having someone shooting at him and that once they got it to Maui, they could add it as an additional offering in their Hawaii for Hawaiians helping hands program.

Brian looked at Joe and said that meant they would accept the yacht.

Joe asked where they would want the repair work to be done.

Brian shook his head and asked if the Coast Guard could tow it to their home base in the Houston area and tie it up at some public pier.

Joe said that he would arrange that to happen.

He then asked if either of them wanted any of the seized homes, other yachts, or gun shops.

Both Brian and Kekoa said no.

Kekoa smiled and added "Just show me the moolah please."

Joe laughed and said that the IRS figured that the "moolah" that he and Brian were likely to received would exceed three billion dollars if they were granted a thirty percent reward on just the money in the Bangkok bank. They had asked Madiline what percentage they should plan to give, and Joe shared that she had replied the entire thirty percent allowed by law and she would have granted more if it was up to her.

After the actions you took representing the IRS, she is a rabid supporter of the two of you. She commented that she was going to show the actions the two of you took during the arrest of Remi as a training video of what good IRS agents can do.

Brian was quite for a few moments and said that he and Kekoa would need to spend some time and figure out how to channel the reward money into good causes around the world. He added that he now saw a few years of doing that versus bringing in the next billionaire.

Joe then said that there was one additional item he had to share. He said that Remi had asked if the two of you could come to the hospital and see him. He said he had an apology and a gift he wanted to give the two of you. He added that if it were OK with the two of them, he would want to be present.

Brian looked over to Kekoa and suggested that they finish eating, drive to New Orleans, visit Remi and then get on the charter and pass out while they flew on the way back to Maui.

Kekoa nodded and said he was all for that plan.

A few hours later, the three of them walked into Remi's hospital room.

Remi raised the top of his bed, so he was sitting upright. He then said that he had been surprised and would never have guessed they were IRS agents.

Brian responded that the world was full of surprises.

Remi then said that he first wanted to thank the two of them for saving his life. He then pointed to Brian and said that he was not going to apologize for having tried to kill him, but he was going to pay amends and wanted to give him the ownership of any of his yachts.

Brian thanked him for his generosity and said that he was choosing the one they had all jumped from after it was repaired.

Remi nodded and said, "done." He added that the "Escape" was his favorite yacht. Then he laughed and said that after failing to ensure his escape perhaps it needed a different name. He then added that he had one additional gift. He said that he wanted the two of them to share ownership of his father's antique gun shop. It only handled antique weapons that were purchased by collectors of rare guns. It enjoyed good sales though it did not make as much money as his other gun shops. He added that it had always been his favorite gun shop.

Brian thanked him for his generosity and then wished him a speedy recovery. He then said that it was time that he start his travel back to Maui.

Remi nodded and added that he wanted Brian to wish his beautiful family the best.

On the way out of the Hospital, Joe looked at Brian and said that he was proud of having him be part of the IRS and then asked why Brian hadn't corrected Remi on any of his misguided thoughts.

Brian replied that Remi did not need to know anything more about Kekoa and himself. Remi seemed content to think that he understood the situation which meant he would spend his time in prison content to leave things the way they were, and he and Kekoa could carry on their lives a little more at ease.

On their return home to Maui Kekoa reminded Brian that the party celebrating his marriage proposal to Anela was that coming Saturday.

Annie was standing at the garage entrance door when Brian walked in. She gave him a hug and commented that she had received an interesting call from a Madiline Westerly who had nothing but praise about the two Hawaiians who had single handedly thwarted an escape by sea by a person who would likely spend many years in prison.

Annie learned about the seventy-five-foot yacht that would soon be docked in Maui. She shook her head and commented that great fortune seemed to be attracted to him like a magnet attracted to iron.

She added that Madiline had agreed on the July date for the trial dealing with the gun running case that was to be opened in Cincinnati. She added that she would be interested in a Maui painting and in giving a donation to Alex's helping hands fund.

The End

<u>About the Author</u>

Ronald E. Mueller
remwriter95@gmail.com

Ron grew up in what is now Flint River State Park in Southeast Iowa. The 170-year-old house Ron lived in is built into a hillside. It faces a 125-foot-high cliff towering over the little Flint River. The house and the land talked to him about; the passing of time, the struggle to conquer the land, the struggles people faced and the wonder of nature.

He climbed the cliffs, crawled into the caves, dove from the swimming rock, collected clams from the bottom of the pond, gigged and skinned frogs for their legs. He trapped muskrats for fur, hunted raccoons in the dead of night, and with only a stick hunted rabbits in the dead of winter.

His young life was outdoors, and nature tested him.

He walked to a one room stone schoolhouse uphill both ways. A stern but warm-hearted teacher, Mrs. Henry was instrumental in shaping his character as she shepherded him from the fourth to the eighth grade. A Montessori before its time. It was a great way to grow up.

His experiences inter-twined with snippets of fantasy lend themselves to the adventures he leads the reader through.

Published by: Around the World Publishing LLC.

QR Links to
ATWP.US web site

Death Broker